The YELLOW-HAMMER'S SONG

A FIRST CENTURY ROMAN SOLDIER SEARCHES FOR TRUTH

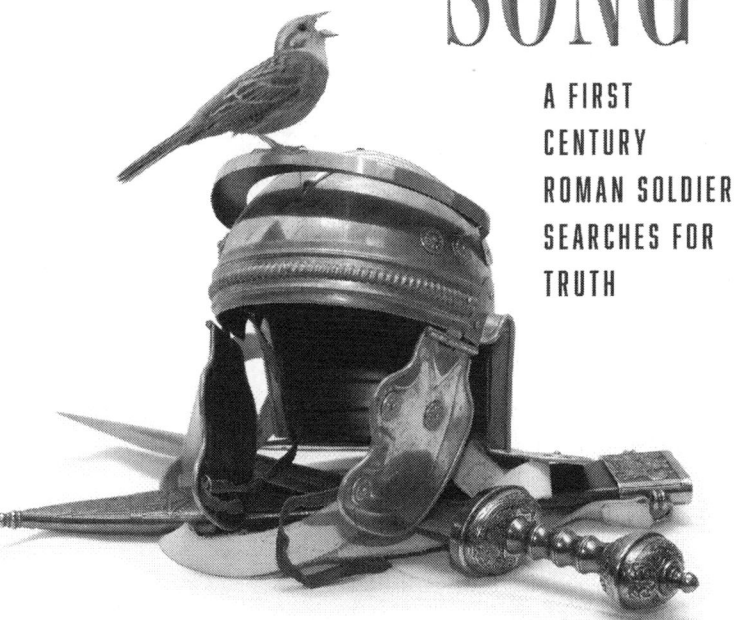

JIM HAMMOND AND C. GRANT WOLF

THE YELLOWHAMMER'S SONG
Copyright © 2022 by Jim Hammond and C. Grant Wolf

All rights reserved. Except for brief quotations in printed reviews, no part of this publication may be reproduced, stored in a retrieval system, or transmitted in any form or by any means (printed, written, photocopied, visual electronic, audio, or otherwise) without the prior permission of the publisher.

Unless otherwise indicated, all Scripture quotations are taken from the (NASB®) New American Standard Bible®, Copyright © 1960, 1971, 1977, 1995, by The Lockman Foundation. Used by permission. All rights reserved. www.lockman.org

Scripture quotations marked (NLT) are taken from the Holy Bible, New Living Translation, copyright ©1996, 2004, 2015 by Tyndale House Foundation. Used by permission of Tyndale House Publishers, Carol Stream, Illinois 60188. All rights reserved.

Print Edition ISBN 13: 979-898604-980-9
Kindle and Epub Editions ISBN: 979-898604-981-6

Cover designed by Daryl Phillips of Daryl Phillips Design, Chattanooga, TN
Editing and interior design by Rick Steele Editorial Services, (https://steeleeditorialservices.myportfolio.com)

Printed in the United States of America

To Jeanie, my bride of 52-plus years who always has been the Wind Beneath My Wings.

–Jim Hammond

In memory of Ruth who, through our nearly 66 years of marriage, truly exemplified a Proverbs 31 wife, and in appreciation of my grandson, Jeremiah Klopfenstein, whose broad literary knowledge and keen eye have been immeasurable in the writing of this book.

–C. Grant Wolf

Contents

Introduction — 1

1. The Soldier — 5
2. The Centurion — 11
3. The Girl — 17
4. The Citadel — 29
5. The Challenge — 33
6. The Mission — 39
7. The Vision — 45
8. The Tanner's House — 49
9. Sleepless in Joppa — 55
10. Peter & Articus — 65
11. The House of Cornelius — 75
12. The Message — 79
13. Centurion's Peace of Heart — 83

TABLE OF CONTENTS

14. The Barracks	87
15. The Conversation	91
16. The Special Friend	97
17. Loss of a Friend	105
18. The Reveal	109
19. Cornelius & Peter	117
20. The Day of the Lord	123
21. Romulus	129
22. Standing in the Dock	143
23. The Crucifixion	149
24. The End…or The Beginning?	157
25. Claudius	163
26. Thomas	169
27. Called by *Yeshua*	179
28. Abigail	191
29. The Attack	197

30. Visions in the Night   201

31. The Physician   205

32. The Leave-Taking   215

33. The Road to Caesarea   219

34. The Journey Home   225

35. The Yellowhammer's Song   235

36. What Shall I Do With *Yeshua*?   247

INTRODUCTION

JIM HAMMOND

For three decades, Grant and I have worked together in the criminal justice system—I in the sheriff's office (most recently as Sheriff of Hamilton County, TN), and Grant with the Chattanooga Police Department as Senior Chaplain. Through the years, both of us have worked together in the Fellowship of Christian Peace Officers-USA.

While serving as a police instructor in Haiti in the late 90s, I saw law enforcement and military personnel from several nations serving together as an occupying force to maintain order and peace in that nation. I realized how similar their challenges were to those of the first-century Roman soldiers who were posted in the Middle East. One day, while reading chapter 10 in the Book of Acts, I began to formulate in my mind how the unnamed soldier who was asked by his commanding officer to bring the apostle Peter back to Caesarea, Philippi from Joppa, Israel would have felt about such a mission. For that soldier, whom we have named *Articus* in the book, it would have been very troubling to bring an uneducated peasant fisherman for a private meeting with a high-ranking Roman centurion.

1

Later, while on a three-year assignment in Jordan helping train Iraqi police in democratic policing, I had the opportunity to experience first-hand the flavor and culture of the Middle East, including that of Israel. Through ancient ruins and exploring the land, I saw first-hand much of what young Articus would have seen and felt: the hot desert winds, sheep, grumbling camels, smells and noises of Bedouin marketplaces, the local flora and fauna, cobblestone streets, and unique architecture. These helped sharpen my senses of what the real-life Bible characters we have fleshed out in *The Yellowhammer's Song* would have experienced and felt. From those experiences and my nearly five decades in law enforcement came the rough draft of this book.

C. GRANT WOLF

After Jim asked me to read the rough draft of his idea about two years ago, I realized he was right—it would make a good historical fiction novel. Combining our joint knowledge of the Bible, Middle Eastern insights Jim gained while living in Jordan, both of our stints in the U.S. military (mine as an occupying soldier in the Far East), a love for presenting Bible truths "outside the box," and my previous experience in writing/editing *Stories of Faith and Courage from Cops on the Street* (AMG Publishers), collaboration just made sense.

As we thought through what Jim had begun while continually adding new material, the text seemed to flow seamlessly. As my grandson, Jeremiah, a master wordsmith observed, he couldn't tell who wrote what. We never had any real disagreements over content or wording, and, with Jeremiah's watchful eye on context, grammar, and historicity, we stayed on key so to speak.

Our desire is for others to find as much joy in reading as we have in writing the novel. Like John Bunyan's *Pilgrim's Progress*, it is packed with biblical and historical references intended to bring life to the characters and relevance to Scripture texts selected from both Old and New Testaments. Whether the reader is a believer in God's Word, is searching for truth like Articus, or simply wants to see Bible stories "between the lines of the text," we believe each will finish *The Yellowhammer's Song* with as much satisfaction as we found in bringing it to life.

CHAPTER

1

THE SOLDIER

"The Lord is a warrior; Yahweh is His Name!"
Exodus 15:3

Articus threw back his warm fleece cover, drew a deep breath followed by an extended yawn, and slowly stretched out his tall, lanky frame. Glancing out the window of the barracks he took note that a new day was just beginning to form with a buttery sun on the horizon rising against a pale blue sky. On the windowsill was perched a small yellow bird which seemed to have its eye on Artie while warbling a sing-song melody that began to go round and round in Artie's mind. But upon being noticed by the young soldier, it fluttered its tiny wings and flew up and away. "Odd," thought Artie, "What an unusual little bird." Then he slowly rose from his sleeping mat, halfway between sleep and wakefulness, shaking the cobwebs from his head. Unsteady on his feet as he fought to keep his eyes open, Artie (as his friends called him) stretched again and did some light calisthenics, still coming to grips with the fact that a new day had begun. As a member of his centurion's personal staff, he did not have to sleep in the general barracks with other young men of his age and rank but was instead housed in special quarters. Thus, he was spared the rude awakening of the morning trumpet blast and extended calisthenics outdoors, whatever the weather. Now that his

5

blood was flowing, and the stiffness removed from his six-foot frame he could think about getting the day started.

Morning was Artie's favorite time of the day. Some of his colleagues disdained the early morning and had no thought of food so early, but Artie relished the prospect of a man-sized breakfast. Fragrant odors from the mess hall wafted through the open window, and his rumbling stomach told him to hurry through his morning ablutions.

In a far corner stood a large stone wash basin filled with water. Servants on duty for the first watch[1] had seen to it that fresh towels hung from wooden pegs, and a large jar of olive oil spiced with the manly fragrance of Agarwood stood ready to freshen the faces and bodies of Roman officers as they prepared for their day's duty. The mild woodsy-scented olive oil invigorated young Artie and brought all his senses alive. After splashing the spiced oil over his body from head to toe and scrubbing it vigorously with a hyssop sponge, he rubbed himself dry with a fresh towel. Admiring his toned lithe body as only a handsome young athlete can, he then began to dress.

Artie fastened his loin cloth around his waist with an engraved leather belt of deer hide. Then he pulled over his head his regimental tunic of woven flax the color of winter grain and slipped his feet into leather sandals imported from the northern provinces, lacing them halfway up his legs to stay in place until bedtime. Finally, he proudly placed a silver amulet symbolic of his military heritage around his tanned and muscular upper left arm and finished by tying his leather coin bag carefully to his belt.

As was his habit in grooming, Artie devoted careful attention to his military appearance. He longed for the day when he proudly would wear the attire of a centurion like his commander, the man who served as his chief mentor and role model. Not given to much humility concerning his abilities and skills, Artie possessed a double dose of pride and vanity. So far as he was concerned, one day the name of Articus Quintus would be spoken of with reverential awe by his fellow soldiers, with great fear by foreign captives, and with much desire and longing by the most beautiful young women of Rome. Without a doubt, the most respected senators in the Roman Forum would offer proud oratories for his unparalleled exploits on behalf of the Roman Empire!

Having completed his grooming and dress, Artie made his way to the mess hall, giving heed to the rumblings of his stomach as it pleaded for morning nourishment. A sampling of figs and meal cakes hot from the stone hearth and sprinkled with wild honey soon filled his plate. A cup of new red wine straight from the finest local vineyard, together with freshly picked pomegranates and succulent melons, would quell the savage beast! A morning person, breakfast was his favorite meal. He always felt rested, fully alive, and ready for a hearty morning meal before he set out to conquer the world!

Seated at a table in the mess hall reserved for the centurion's personal staff, Artie joined in light-hearted banter with colleagues already there. Discussions ranged from the day's assignments to last night's entertainment in the local taverns, sporting events, local eateries, and tales of having been in the arms of one of the town's local raven-haired beauties. Though he too was a young man with all the desires of youth, Artie's sense of duty to country, loyalty to Caesar, and respect for his centurion, impelled him to curb those desires while he climbed the ladder of success in the Roman Army. Artie relished his position as a special attendant to such a high-ranking official as his centurion, and he didn't want to do anything to jeopardize that. It was a special and almost-unheard-of honor for an officer as young as he to be posted to work directly for such an honored centurion. As devoted as he was to the Empire, Artie was equally loyal and devoted to his centurion.

Sated by the ample nourishment, Artie finished dressing by attaching his dagger sheath to his belt and checking his coin pouch to make sure he had enough Roman and Israeli coins for any purchases he might make that day. Though Roman coins were the official coin of the realm, some Israelis preferred the coins used when Israel was an independent nation.[2] *Those prideful Jews,* he mused, *Why can't they just accept all the greatness Rome has to offer?*

That thought left Artie's mind as he contemplated the good life of a Roman legionnaire. Proud of his Roman citizenship and filled with the strength of youth and a passion for life, his dreams of the future ahead were as intoxicating to him as vintage wine is to an old man seeking solace of mind and freedom from the afflictions and sorrows of age. Even so, he couldn't help but wonder how he got posted as a special attendant to such a respected centurion. Surely there were experienced young officers with greater family connections and political position than he. In fact, Artie could see no logical reason for his being so honored. And why Caesarea? He felt sure his posting to this port city named for the great Augustus Caesar was arranged by his family mentor. But Caesarea was certainly not a first-choice duty assignment for a young officer longing to engage in the mighty military battles with the legions that even then were crushing the enemies of Rome. Still, he knew the political influence his superior held with powerful men in Rome would serve to advance a junior officer's career toward rank and privilege. This made him question his present posting all the more. One day he hoped to be posted to Rome, for that is where real power and influence resided. Did not the entire world proclaim that all roads lead to Rome? That is where one day he would be known and respected as one of the nation's finest officers.

Artie's final act before leaving his quarters was to don his helmet. When dressed in full uniform with its plumage flowing in the breeze, Artie felt great pride marching with his company to the admiration of the thousands who lined the Appian way cheering on the victorious soldiers of Rome. He would be even prouder after a local tradesman of fine plumage would retrofit it with the largest and most colorful feathers of the blue Ostrich of Gad. "I must get that done today," he thought as he headed for that day's duty assignment.

Notes

1. Each day and night was divided into four watches: first watch, six to nine o'clock; second, nine to twelve; third, twelve to three; and fourth, three to six.
2. When Israel was an independent nation, Jews were opposed to any coinage having an image of an earthly ruler. In paying the Temple tax they would use the *half shekel*, which portrayed no such ruler. Generally, Romans used the *denarius*, which was made of silver and represented one day's salary. Money exchangers made a handsome profit changing the denarius to half shekels so Jews could pay their taxes.

CHAPTER

2

THE CENTURION

"Now there was a man at Caesarea named Cornelius, a centurion of what ws called the Italian cohort."

Acts 10:1

The duties of a centurion in occupied territory require a combination of quiet diplomacy, a firm hand, and a sharp sword. Designated as Keeper of the Peace, a centurion's role is to balance the interests of the Empire with the need to pacify the citizens of a conquered nation. On one hand there must be sufficient military force to impress the awesome power of Rome upon the local citizens. However, when called for, there needs to be a light touch to keep disgruntled citizens who feel unduly oppressed from aggressively choosing to fight and die rather than endure subjugation. This political balancing act has to be carried out under the edicts of career politicians who are appointed as proconsuls, procurators, and governors because of their favoritism with Rome. Family connections, wealth, and political pressure often lead to some of the most-inept of men being given appointments to rule over conquered nations and peoples such as these Hebrews.

Sitting alone in his office, the centurion contemplated the twenty years he had given his life in service to Rome. Those years—plus three major military campaigns and two life-threatening injuries—had earned him the rank of centurion. Such are the rewards of a man who had devoted his life to Rome as a man of the sword. Time and the daily hardships of living had seasoned him. His aquiline nose spoke to his pure Roman heritage. Muscular and well-tanned, sporting thick curly hair tinged with silver and trimmed in the traditional short-cropped style found among Caesar's well-groomed officers, Cornelius's face was etched with the weathered lines of numerous hard-fought battles, countless miles of marching, nights spent with little sleep, and meals of short rations. His dark penetrating eyes, deep and mysterious, signaled to those who gazed into them a man who knew hardship, terrors of battle, and the tragedy of seeing too many brave young men thrust into war, only to be struck down and buried on foreign soil. Yet, these same eyes radiated warmth, a compassion for others, and a love for life and the empire he had sworn to serve and protect.

A disciplined man of iron, Cornelius also was a man given to abundant displays of generosity and charity. Since his posting to this city on the Mediterranean coast some seventy miles from Jerusalem, the seat of Jewish civil and religious power, he had become very interested in the religion of the Jews. He found the Jewish people to be highly religious, controversial, and most unusual in their passionate belief there was only one God. Such a thing was unheard of among Romans. As a young lad growing up in the shadow of the Coliseum, the centurion had not paid much attention to religion. Still, as a soldier, especially during times of battle, he would call for assistance from all the gods of his family and any other god he happened to think of at the time. But when those times were over and his energy had returned, he would retreat to his self-reliance and tell himself again that religion was for the aged, infirm, and those who feared that great unknown, death; just something to give solace to those who were too weak and had lost their own resolve. All a centurion like him really needs is his sword, his javelin, and his cunning skill as a warrior; that and the power of Rome at his back.

Still, in recent years he had sensed a change in his attitude and feelings about a divine presence in life and the world. The steady advancement of his own years had mellowed him somewhat, and he found that more often lately he was questioning life, its meaning, and its purpose. The centurion loved his own family dearly and even felt a genuine compassion for the people of this conquered land. He considered himself a blessed man and often gave to those less fortunate. After years of war and conquests for Caesar, being charitable gave him a great deal of satisfaction. More importantly, he had begun a serious search for answers to his questions about life. He often pondered the concept of only one god. If indeed there was only one universal god, what would that god want or expect from such a medaled and high-ranking centurion as he?

Prayer seldom plays a part in the life of a man of the sword. Oh, certainly one always says a little entreaty to the gods when encountering hostilities, not knowing if one's name might be on the edge of a sword, the tip of a hurtling javelin, or the point of the archer's arrow. His own experience had taught him how quickly one's prayers become earnest after tasting the raw savage power of metal thrust against flesh. Twice in his long and often dangerous career he had experienced the searing pain of torn flesh and the smell of his own blood and had been gripped with the fear of impending death. Both times a certain earnest evaluation of his life and recognition of what was truly important were quickly set in motion. Property acquired, ribbons won, or worldly passions never rush to the forefront of one's mind during such traumatic events. More often than not, what the mind focuses on sharply has more to do with relationships…words left unsaid to loved ones, opportunities missed to do good or to be kind, and a desire to feel at peace with the world.

His first experience with death came when he was a young officer fighting in the battle of lower Sparta. Even now, after all these many years, his mind still could bring into sharp detail every vivid moment of the event.

As his regiment advanced on that long-ago field of battle, javelins poised to strike, he came face to face with an enemy archer whose countenance was frighteningly brutish. He was a big man with thick arms and legs, like the trunks of the ancient cedars of Lebanon. His bloodthirsty eyes danced with raw hatred, and the snarl on his lips spoke of utter contempt for all soldiers of the Empire. He emitted a raw savage roar that chilled the young warrior to the bone. The powerful bow clasped in his hands was drawn to full tautness, the point of its armament personifying death itself. Whether by reflex of his own expert training or from desperate fright, the centurion was not sure, but he threw his own javelin at the exact moment his opponent released his death arrow. With a hollow thud the javelin scored a direct hit in the center mass of the hapless archer's chest. But in his haste to deliver his own deadly missile, the centurion had unconsciously lowered his shield, momentarily exposing his left side to the enemy's arrow. It was a painful mistake he realized all too soon.

Reeling from the searing blow of the projectile as it tore through his flesh, the young soldier staggered back, momentarily losing his footing. Though his knees buckled, he managed to right himself and quickly recovered his shield of protection. The arrow had penetrated just above his leather belt on his left side, exiting through the fleshy part without striking anything vital. The raw angry wound oozed blood onto his torn tunic. So far as he could tell no bones, ribs, or vital organs appeared to be compromised, but the pain was excruciating. He had often heard soldiers talk of encounters with an archer's arrows on fields of battle. Such testimonials often describe being able to observe the projectile as if in slow motion hurtling toward its intended victim. The razor point would become clearly visible, as did the quivering flex of the wood shaft and the rustle of the stabilizing feather. Even the sound of the arrow's "swoosh" through the air seemed to advance slowly as it sought its mark. Victims of such attacks often spoke of a sense of being disassociated from the scene as it played out before them. This also was his own experience, quickly followed by waves of piercing pain and an overwhelming feeling of nausea as he smelled his own blood soaking his tunic.

A quick glance at his opponent left no doubt that this archer would fight no more. His bow was discarded at his feet, while both his dirty callused hands—now stained bright red with his own blood—tightly clasped the shaft of the javelin embedded deep within his chest. His eyes no longer flashed with the hatred and anger of a few minutes ago, but now reflected the horror of his own impending death. He was a dead man standing. Even though similar scenes of death would be repeated often over the years, the pleading eyes of that foe with their desperation and hopelessness would remain forever with the centurion.

Lately, something else had been troubling his spirit. More and more he began to feel there was a spiritual aspect to life. His youthful sense of immortality had waned, and he realized that religion was playing a more active role in his life. He found he was beginning to embrace religion with the same fervor with which he approached his career as a dedicated servant to Caesar. His own family observed that he had become devoutly pious and zealous in his devotion to prayer and worship. He appeared sincerely to be seeking to know about "gods." Something inside him suggested that the Jews might be right when they spoke of "only one god." Strangely enough, it seemed there was just something natural about there being only "one god. After all, there was just one Caesar he served, and nature taught him that only one physical father had given him life. For a man trained all his life to follow orders and to serve one master, it made little sense to acknowledge the many gods the Romans worshiped, all demanding allegiance to them—and then there was the strange encounter that very day about three o'clock in the afternoon....[1]

Notes

1. Acts 10:3

CHAPTER

3

THE GIRL

"How beautiful you are! Your eyes are like doves behind your veil; Your hair is like a flock of goats that have descended from Mount Gilead."

Song of Solomon 4:1

The desert sun cast shimmering waves of heat on the crowded streets of Caesarea as Artie haggled with the plumage tradesman.

"Are you positive this is the finest feather you have? The price you quoted would buy an entire Ostrich!"

"Sir, there is no finer feather in the entire region, and you are getting it for the same price I would ask the Emperor himself!"

Finally, the negotiating was over, a price agreed upon, and a completion date set for one week. Force of habit led Artie to pause a moment to survey the street in both directions while leaving the open-air stall. After turning to his left, he leisurely began to make his way through the narrow streets. A plethora of nations and cultures crowded the central marketplace and mixed freely with one other, creating a kaleidoscopic montage of sights, sounds, and smells of city life. Some were hawking their wares to no one in particular, while others were deep in animated conversation, haggling over price and quality of a variety of goods. Young children held tightly to their mothers' clothing while older youngsters ran among the stalls and carts playing children's games like "hide and seek" or "tag, you're it." In addition to the arguments over price and quality could be heard angry discussions that prices and the ever-present dreaded taxes were getting too high, especially those levied by the Roman government. Artie pretended not to hear remarks deriding Rome. Though he had the authority to mete out punishment for those who complained too loudly, sometimes it was best to let some things go. He considered how he might feel if the situation was reversed, and if he was living under an occupying force. *I'd probably do more than just blow off a little steam,* he thought. Besides, he was off-duty and not about to let a bit of local politics break his enjoyment of the day.

Though Caesarea was not the post he had hoped for, Artie still loved its hustle and bustle. There was something about its tantalizing smells of fresh herbs, spices, and peppery contents of cooking pots, combined with the pungent odor of fresh straw and flax. The earthy smell of animals and wood smoke and, yes, even the smell of humanity added to the rich mixture of life in this blended city. Funny how smells can bring memories of times and places long past. Sometimes he would catch just a hint of fragrance in the air that would remind him of a raven-haired girl he once knew or of a place he had traveled since his conscription into the Roman military. Though still a young man, he already had seen much of the Roman Empire's vast diversity. He considered himself a fortunate young man, blessed by the gods, if any really existed.

While his own family had embraced the usual divinities of Rome, he long had harbored doubts about gods and religion—though he wasn't quite ready to abandon the idea all together. One fact he did know: he was a devout follower of the Caesar as his lord and master. Who was he to doubt what he had been told: that Caesar was a god or at least favored by the gods as the one to rule Rome.

Just then his thoughts were interrupted as he passed by a synagogue, the local place of worship for the Jews. He observed a crowd gathered around a man who seemed to have captured the attention of all present. Always alert to the possibility of radical groups who might attempt to subvert the authority of Rome, the young soldier deviated from his path for a moment to check out the situation. As he approached, he overheard the man speak…

"I was resting when an Angel of *Yahweh* spoke directly to me and told me to go south to the road that descends from Jerusalem to Gaza. I did as I had been instructed and found a court official of Candace, Queen of the Ethiopians, riding in his chariot. He had been to Jerusalem to worship and was returning home, reading from one of our sacred scrolls, when the *Holy Spirit* told me directly: 'Go up and join this chariot.' Seeing him there in his expensive chariot, I couldn't help but think of how King Solomon's chariot was described, made from timbers of Lebanon with posts of silver, back of gold and its seat of purple fabric.[1] I knew how important he must be and was more than a little hesitant to force myself on him. But when I saw he was reading from the prophet *Isaiah*, I asked if he understood what he was reading. You can imagine my astonishment when he said, 'No. How can I unless someone guides me?' and then invited me to get in and sit beside him to explain what the prophet had written."[2]

Artie immediately recognized the speaker as one Phillip the Evangelist, a Jew, who was part of the religious sect known as "The Way." This man was one of several individuals Rome watched closely due to their radical notions and impassioned speeches. To Artie's way of thinking, men like Phillip probably were mentally unstable and could be a real danger to Rome. "The Way" claimed their god was three-gods-in-one who had for a time possessed a human body and lived here on the earth. The danger this posed was how Phillip and his group infuriated their fellow Jews by saying that this man-god, *Yeshua*, was the Jew's hoped-for *Messiah*. On more than one occasion, Artie and his colleagues had to quell civil disturbances caused by these promoters of "The Way." As he listened carefully to Phillip, Artie couldn't help but think, *These Jews sure have a lot of zeal!*

Phillip continued…

"I could tell the man was searching for something in the Scriptures but couldn't understand what Isaiah meant when he wrote: '*He was led like a sheep to the slaughter, and as a lamb before the shearer is silent, so he did not open his mouth. In his humiliation he was deprived of justice. Who can speak of His descendants? For His life was taken from the earth.*'[3] Then this Ethiopian official put this question to me: 'Tell me, please, who is the prophet Isaiah talking about, himself or someone else?'"

"I was excited to hear his question. After a quick silent prayer to *Yahweh* for wisdom I took the man's document and beginning with that very passage in *Isaiah*, I explained in detail the good news about *Yeshua*[4]; I didn't leave out a thing. Citing prophet after prophet I gave him the good news of how *Yahweh* knows we are all sinners and need a way to reach heaven since we will never be able to be good enough or can do enough on our own for *Yahweh* to accept us into paradise. I spoke to this official about how *Yeshua* Himself took on the flesh of man, born to a young virgin who had never had relations with a man. This allowed *Yeshua* to present Himself as a perfect example of holiness and become a sinless sacrifice for the sins of humanity. I explained that *Yeshua* became the perfect "Lamb of God" as a sacrifice, as opposed to the lambs that are used in sacrifice now to symbolize the need for something or someone to pay for our sins.[5] *Yeshua* was the only one who—being God Himself without sin—could give His life as a perfect sacrifice so that never again will temporary sacrifices have to be made. I helped this man understand that by accepting what *Yeshua* had done for him on the cross he could rest in eternal peace, knowing that no matter what life throws at him, he would have *Yahweh* as his help and comfort. He could enjoy life here on earth and eternity in heaven with all others who trust *Yeshua* as their savior."[6]

Artie furrowed his brow as he thought intensely at those words. Such a thing was impossible! This man's talk was crazy. How could a virgin conceive a child without the seed of man placed into her womb? Could a god become flesh and take on the sins of other people so they might be assured of paradise in another life after death? Would such a god want to do this? If so, why? Could he as a Roman soldier be accepted by such a god? The thought of only one god and that god becoming a man just so he could die for other people didn't make any sense, especially since those people didn't seem to care one way or the other what their god did. "Strange" was all he could think. He recalled a saying his old school master used to repeat often: "It takes many people of diverse thoughts to make up the world." *How true*, Artie thought, especially "all kinds of strange people." Still, it was an interesting concept and something about which he felt he would like to know more.

The gathering of Jews and words of Phillip seemed harmless enough, but Artie was concerned how Philip's words of *Yeshua* being "god" could make them so mad. Like other members of "The Way," Phillip seemed to blame the Jewish leaders for *Yeshua's* crucifixion, but as far as Artie could see, it was the carpenter's own fault. Artie had heard that *Yeshua* had claimed to be King of the Jews, and that he and his followers were trying to incite the Jews against Rome. He even heard that some had declared that *Yeshua* had claimed to be the rightful king instead of Caesar. You would think that *Yeshua's* death would have put the matter to rest; that he was not their self-proclaimed "Messiah."[7] Artie made a mental note to inform the garrison to watch this Phillip more closely.

Still pondering those thoughts, Artie resumed his leisurely stroll through the dusty, winding narrow streets bustling with hawkers, merchants, buyers, sellers, the very young and the very old. In addition, there were the ever-present beggars soliciting alms.

A string of camels laden with bulging packs stood idly by a stone cistern in the open square. Each camel was tended by a young nomadic lad who, no doubt, had brought these ships of the desert there to drink their fill for some long journey ahead. Camels are odd creatures. Their sleepy, doe eyes are overshadowed by long eyelashes that are the envy of many Arab women. But their beautiful eyelashes are somewhat disarming to anyone who does not know their nasty dispositions. These temperamental creatures are especially prone to spitting, biting, slobbering and sometimes administering painful kicks to unsuspecting victims. Besides that, they stink. Despite all that, Artie found these beasts of burden a necessary though barely tolerable mode of transportation. Their continual groans, growls, and grunts give never-ending evidence of their ill disposition. Watching these desert cargo-carriers drink their fill reminded him of his own thirst. He noticed a nearby vendor's stall where hung a watering jar. A large cylinder-shaped jug, slender at the top and base but bulging in the middle, it was made of clay and covered in animal hide. To keep whatever it contained cool, it was soaked from time to time in water. As the water evaporated from the hide, it cooled the water in the jug to produce a refreshing drink for any thirsty shopper. Artie filled a wooden dipper hanging beside it and proceeded to drink deeply of the cool liquid, allowing some to spill down his neck to lightly soak his tunic and enjoy some of the same cooling effect on his skin. Water containers like this were for the general public's use, often serving to attract customers to a vendor's merchandise.

The stall where the water jug was located contained mountains of fresh fruit, large juicy oranges, succulent melons, and ruby red apples. A young urchin in tattered clothes stood by the table, transfixed by the display before him. His stringy matted hair, smudged face, and wide brown eyes were mute evidence it had been some time since the boy had eaten anything, much less fresh fruit. Feeling a strange stirring of compassion for the lad, he selected a rather large sun-ripened orange, stooped down, held the orange on the tips of his fingers and thumb and presented it to the boy. Startled by the sudden presence of a Roman soldier squatting beside him, the boy's eyes filled with terror, and he froze on the spot. Artie just smiled and gestured that it was alright for the lad to take the offering.

"Here my young friend, a gift to you from me. Please take it as from one friend to another."

The boy hesitated, furtively glancing back-and-forth from the officer to the orange, fearful and not sure what to do. Finally, his desire for the fruit overcame his fear, and he quickly took the offering while backing away from Artie without saying a word.

Nearby, Artie heard a merchant announce a new supply of lamps in various sizes and shapes, complete with wool wicks and clay flasks purported to be filled with the purest of olive oil, especially mixed for smokeless burning. The man guaranteed they were the brightest burning lamps in town. What really caught Artie's attention was the young woman standing next to the merchant.

She had been watching him interact with the boy, but when she saw that he had noticed her, she quickly diverted her eyes and began arranging the lamps on a fine woven carpet, carefully placing each one in just the right position to create eye appeal to customers passing nearby. She was a dark-haired beauty with skin the color of golden honey and the most beautiful green eyes Artie had ever seen. She wore a simple ankle-length dress which clung to her petite but very lovely form. Her small feet were bare, identifying her as working class. But there was something about this lovely creature that conveyed both character and dignity. In that brief first encounter Artie felt a stirring in his chest like he never before had felt. When he caught her looking and then shyly turning her head away, he felt compelled to know who this lovely creature was.

Artie replaced the water dipper, paid for the young boy's orange, who was still in a state of shock, tousled the lad's hair, and causally drifted over to the lamp seller's stall. Standing tall and straight with his chest extended a bit, he examined first one then another of the array of lamps, feigning interest in making a purchase but hoping to strike up a conversation with the beautiful young woman. "Have these lamps been tempered properly?" he asked, while smiling flirtatiously and trying to take in all her beauty without being too obvious.

"Of course, Sir. My uncle is the finest lamp maker within three days journey of this city. His reputation is such that several times a year we travel from Jerusalem to Caesarea to meet the needs of our customers here. I, myself, help prepare the special clay, using only the best ingredients to add strength and smoothness. My family raises the olives for the oil they burn and oversees the entire rendering process from start to finish."

Stalling for time, Artie said "Let me see that one over there with two wicks, the blue one. I need one that will furnish strong light for long dark nights. When one is by himself at night, having a bright lamp can make it feel less lonely." At this comment the young woman smiled shyly, casting her eyes to the ground as she turned to retrieve the requested lamp. Handing it carefully to him, their hands touched ever so slightly, but it was enough for Artie to feel the warmth of her delicate and soft hand. In turn, with the back of her hand she brushed her long silken hair away from her face, demurely returning his smile with her own, but with a blush and downcast eyes. Though the exchange had been brief, the electric shock which had run through his body gave him feelings he never had felt before; he desperately wanted to know more about this innocently beautiful young woman! He was about to ask her name when the vendor spoke: "Abigail, tend to the donkey and bring me that flask of oil. I also will need the five shekels your brother gave you." "Yes uncle, right away," she replied. *Abigail*, thought Artie. *I'll never forget that name.*

Abigail moved quickly to attend to her uncle's request, but after a few steps she glanced back to see if the officer was watching her. He was, which caused her smile to produce a hint of a dimple in the corner of her lovely mouth. "Wow," thought Artie. "I definitely need to purchase more lamps shaped by the hands of this lovely creature." Before he could figure out his next move, he caught sight of a regimental messenger headed his way. "Soldier of Rome," declared the messenger, "I've been searching for you everywhere. Your centurion requests your immediate presence. I carry official correspondence direct from my lord's hand. It must be a matter of great importance for I received instructions from him personally and was ordered to make utmost haste to bring this document to your attention."

As he reached for the dispatch, Artie gave another glance in the girl's direction. By then she had disappeared, which caused a strange sensation and sadness in him from not knowing more about her. However, "duty called," and no doubt this picture of loveliness would be long gone before he could return to seek her out. *No use in inquiring more about her from her uncle*, he thought, for the man did not seem pleased at all to have a Roman soldier's attention bestowed on his niece.

After dismissing the courier, Artie stepped into the shadow of an arched doorway, away from prying eyes. Satisfied that he was alone, he opened the scroll sealed with the official wax signet of Rome and proceeded rapidly to scan the document. The news was unnerving:

He was to report for a special assignment.

He was to undertake a journey for an unknown purpose.

The trip was extremely important.

He would receive details from his centurion when he returned to the Citadel.

With such an urgent message Artie spent no more time wandering about the market or listening to the idle chatter of zealots quoting religious writings of the Jews. But he couldn't get out of his mind the girl's beauty or fragrance she wore.

Notes

1. Song of Solomon 3:9–10
2. Acts 8:26-28
3. Isaiah 53:7-8
4. The letter "j" did not come into use until the mid-1500's. For that reason, to stay in historical context, this novel uses the common name for Jesus in the first century (AD), *Yeshua*. (And we are using the Hebrew name for God, *Yahweh*.) However, to avoid confusion for the reader, we are using the letter "j" for other common words like Jerusalem, Judea, Jews, etc.
5. Leviticus Chapter 5
6. Acts 8:28–39
7. John 4:26

CHAPTER

4

THE CITADEL

"All the walls were of costly stone cut according to measure, sawed with saws, inside and outside; even from the foundation to the coping and on the outside to the great court."

1 Kings 7:9

Articus loved the grandeur of the Citadel at Caesarea. Built in the style of the ancient Jewish kings, its size and height loomed over all the other important buildings of the city. Everyone, from lowly Jewish peasants to the most powerful aristocrats, understood immediately that this was the seat of power over all in that region.

Taking the stone steps two-at-a-time, Artie entered the Citadel through the North Gate, the one reserved for ranking officials. His posting gave him many special privileges, including being able to pass through this reserved gate. Others were required to enter and exit through the lower gate, always difficult to navigate due to the large number of beggars, merchants, vendors, women of ill repute, gamblers, and the general populace who plied their various trades or brought complaints and requests to the soldiers of the garrison.

Upon reaching the second floor, he paused outside the massive doors of the regimental headquarters. Taking a moment to adjust his dagger belt, straighten his tunic, and assume proper military bearing, the young man drew a quick deep breath before delivering one sharp rap on the door and entering the room quickly with military precision.

Rather large and impressive by military standards, the room was tastefully decorated with man-sized furniture and a large quantity of accent pieces, reminiscent of the government offices in Rome. One had the distinct feeling this not only was an important official's domain, but also a testimony to his military exploits. Several styles of shields, broadswords, javelins, lances, and spears lined the south wall, and an imposing replica of the great Roman Shield graced a large portion of the room's north wall. Below this awe-inspiring symbol of might and glory stood a magnificent hand-carved oak table of Mesopotamian design.

Cluttered with numerous scrolls, documents, quills, parchments and an ornate inkwell, this elaborate table no doubt had been privy to many highly secret conversations, official letters, and state documents. Other items of furniture included several straight-back chairs, two Roman couches, and many stands holding brass lamps of Turkish design that gave flickering light and warmth to even the shadowy corners of the room. In a far corner stood a heavy wooden washstand with an alabaster basin and a tall pitcher of the same material. Two towels folded in precise military style were placed next to them. A thick Persian carpet covered a large portion of the stone floor. Treasured for their high quality, rich colors, and intricate designs, carpets like these were found only in the homes or offices of very wealthy and influential individuals. In addition to the impressive symbol of Roman power on the wall and the finely crafted desk, one other item commanded the full attention of first-time visitors to this centurion's office: a larger-than-life bust of Augustus Caesar, the grand emperor. The sculpture stood on a marble column, carefully placed to be bathed in light from the east windows of the Citadel. With cold steely eyes and a stern brow, this visage of Caesar was an unmistakable likeness of the emperor himself. There was no doubt the man was a powerful ruler and grand emperor of the known civilized world.

Artie never tired of being in this magnificent office. Its very presence spoke of power and grandeur. It had the look, feel and leathery smell of a man's world. Though the room was large, it was not so much its size as it was the aura it seemed to exude. To Artie it bespoke of the centurion who occupied the room, a man who in many ways had become the father the young warrior had never known.

Artie's father, also a centurion, had died in service to Rome. He had heard of his father's many exploits, but because he was gone from home much of the time on military deployments, it was not until Artie's own assignment to Caesarea that he discovered Cornelius had served with his father. From the moment of that revelation, he hungered to acquire any scrap of information he could about his father. But protocol demanded that he not be too familiar with a superior, making him hesitant to probe for much information. At times Artie even found himself fantasizing that his own father really was not dead, and one day they might serve together. Though this was just a young man's wishful daydream, he longed for a relationship which never could be, and he couldn't think of any better father figure than the man he called "my centurion."

CHAPTER

5

THE CHALLENGE

"Cornelius, a centurion, a righteous and God-fearing man well-spoken of by the entire nation of the Jews, was divinely directed by a holy angel to send for you to come to his house and hear a message from you."

Acts 10:22

The man in whose presence the young officer stood spoke not a word but continued reading a scroll, stopping from time to time to dip a quill in ink and carefully post a note on the document. Finally, the centurion laid the quill down on the desk, lowered the parchment, and lifted his eyes toward the young officer. He cleared his throat and spoke: "At ease, soldier, be seated. I am about to describe an unusual event that occurred here today in this very room, and then ask that you undertake a special mission on my personal behalf."

Taken aback both in the way the centurion spoke and the lack of customary protocol by his superior, Artie hesitated a brief moment before finding the appropriate place to settle his lanky frame, a chair of modest size and proportion constructed of cedar of Lebanon, noted for its strength, durability, and suitability for displaying the maker's craftsmanship.

As every career soldier knows, the command of a general officer to be "at ease" is not the same as one coming from a lesser superior. Outwardly, Artie tried to appear somewhat relaxed, but he remained seated "ramrod-straight" with his right hand holding his helmet on his right knee and his left hand resting on his other knee, as though expecting any moment to be brought to full attention.

His commander began to speak: "Articus, I am going to speak to you with complete candor, asking you to hear me out without judgment or thinking I am a man who has taken leave of my senses from too many battles fought or head wounds received. Though you may surely think me mad for what I am about to reveal to you, please be patient while I recount a very strange happening from earlier this day.

"As you know, Rome has assigned me the responsibility of overseeing the protection of this city and all her people. I take my duties most seriously and to the best of my ability have performed every task assigned. In the process I have come to love this city and her people.

"My family and I have worked diligently to be accepted as members of this community and to be involved in community life. We give to charity, take part in local public functions, and even have contributed to the care and construction of local centers of Jewish worship. It is to this latter activity that I wish to direct your attention.

"You might think it strange that a man of the sword such as I should speak of worship and religion. Perhaps it is because all my life I have been a man of the sword, having witnessed the sorrows and hopelessness which come when a man's life ends on the battlefield. As I near the end of both my career and my days on this earth, I increasingly have begun to seek an answer to this question, 'Is there a reason for this world and life in general, and specifically does my own life really have meaning and purpose?'

"For some time, I have puzzled over the reality of gods. Earnestly I have sought to know if there is only one god over all men, as the Jews believe, or if there are many gods to whom we owe allegiance, as we Romans are taught. Lately I have felt strongly there really can be but one supreme being, and that he is the only god who exists. To that end, I have devoted myself to prayer and fasting in an attempt to know who this god is and what he requires of me. In addition to my regular prayers, at times I also give alms to those in need, hoping my good deeds will help me find meaning and purpose in my life."

Artie felt very uncomfortable at hearing the intimate private thoughts of his superior and even more uncomfortable witnessing such vulnerability from his mentor. He was not sure he wanted to hear that his superior felt the need to rely on anything or anyone for his strength other than himself and the power of Rome. He certainly did not wish to entertain thoughts that this powerful man experienced doubts and fears like those of lesser, ordinary men. Since coming to Caesarea he often had told himself, "If I can become half the man my centurion is, then I will overcome my own doubts and fears." Now the man he had made "his god" was making him nervous.

Artie remained quiet and attentive while the centurion continued. "Earlier today I was here in my office praying that I might know the reality of the true god. Then, without warning, I distinctly saw a man standing before me unlike any man I had ever seen. His penetrating eyes, his poise, his confidence, and his demeanor gave him a presence that is hard to describe. That presence seemed to fill this entire room, and I felt completely helpless. Even though I never before had encountered an angel, the emanation coming from him caused me to know without conversation that this was not a man but an angel. When he spoke, he called me by my name and seemed to know all about me.

"For a moment I could not believe my eyes or ears. I just stared and simultaneously experienced fear, peace, and awe. Neither my legs nor my arms were of any use to me at that moment, and I dared not to draw a breath. I am not sure how I managed, but I finally stammered to the angel, 'What is it you wish, my Lord?'

"That mighty being then told me that my sincere prayers and gifts to the poor had been heard and seen by God, and that I was to send for a man some distance away in another city. I was instructed to have that man brought here to learn from him the truth about my questions of God and life.[1]

"Now Articus, right about now you must be thinking to yourself that this is the ramblings of a madman. I can't blame you if you think I have taken leave of my senses and should be relieved of my duty, but I trust you will let me continue.

"Son, if I have served you well as your superior, mentor, and centurion, then I call upon you now to serve me in my desire to know the truth of what this heavenly visitation means."

Artie felt his own military bearing undermined as his shoulders slumped and his head slowly lowered to his chest. His eyes stared at the floor as his mind raced to make sense of the conversation his ears had just received.

Seated before him was the man who had attained hero status in Artie's mind. His centurion was a "man's man" who knew no fear and feared no man. Yet, in but a few brief moments, he had confessed to the same fears and weaknesses common to all mortals. Artie was aware that his centurion prayed and that he and his family were known to practice religion, but Artie had also assumed that was just part of the public duties expected of all government officials. For men like the Roman Commandant of Caesarea, community participation like this was "the social thing to do" to help people feel less antagonistic toward the occupiers who oversaw their very way of life. It made good political sense to be seen as their friend. Artie had never thought for one minute that his superior officer really could be that serious about religion or have doubts and concerns about the purpose of life or thoughts of death and beyond.

Momentarily, a pall of silence hung in the air like an impenetrable cloud after Cornelius finished speaking. Each stared quietly at the other. The centurion loved the young man seated in front of him like his own son. The young warrior reminded him of his own early days of service to the Empire. As Cornelius once had been—full of life, vigor and vitality— Articus was the future of the Roman Army. Yet soon enough, the lad would know the troubles of life and infirmities of age. Battles would be fought, comrades would die, blood would be spilled, colleagues would betray, lovers would disappoint, troubles would come, and at the end, death would steal in unannounced. He thought of something he had read in a Jewish scroll: "*Vanity of vanities, says the Preacher; Vanity of vanities, all is vanity. What profit has a man from all his labor in which he toils under the sun? One generation passes away, and another generation comes; but the earth abides forever.*"[2] It did not take an educated man long to understand these simple words. All things in life come to naught in the end, for man is born, lives but a short time, and then returns to nothingness. All his striving to be rich, famous, and loved is futility. One generation comes to replace another, and so on for years past and years to come. Indeed, what does it profit? One could not take to the grave a single thing. The centurion seemingly had come to realize that without the hope of a true God, a future eternal life was indeed vanity.

Finally, the young warrior slowly raised his head, stood to his feet, threw his shoulders back, and in his best regimental posture announced to his commanding officer, "Sir, I am ready to carry out the orders of Rome and my centurion. What would you have me do, SIR?"

The centurion studied Artie's face for some time before finally speaking: "It is not for Rome or Caesar that I ask for your participation in this task, Articus. Rather, it is for me as your mentor and friend. I need the aid of a trusted confidant to accompany two of my servants to the house of a certain man located a day's journey from here. There you will find the individual with whom I must speak. Can I count on you to handle this delicate matter for me?"

Notes

1. Acts 10:1-8
2. Ecclesiastes 1:2–4

CHAPTER

6

THE MISSION

"'Now send men to Joppa, and send for Simon whose surname is Peter. He is lodging with Simon, a tanner, whose house is by the sea. He will tell you what you must do.' Cornelius called two of his household servants and a devout soldier from among those who waited on him continually. When he had explained all these things to them, he sent them to Joppa."

Acts 10:5–8

Except for the sound of crunching sand and pebbles under foot, the three men walked in silence, each lost in his own thoughts. The noonday sun blazed from a cloudless sky. An intense brightness radiated upon the dry landscape, barren except for occasional scrub brush, stones, and rocks bleached bone white, and a few gnarled trees, worn and weather beaten by hot desert winds blowing in from the distant sea. Small flocks of sheep were dotted here and there, with a few black goats leisurely nibbling their way among the thorny scrub patches. Under an ancient acacia tree sat an old man, staff resting on his crossed legs, perhaps daydreaming of his youth long passed. He appeared to be stoking a small smoky fire surrounded by flat stones on which rested a blackened spouted teapot, whose content no doubt was flavored with local herbs. *These nomadic sheep herders are a dirty lot,* thought Artie. They wore rough-hewn clothing (no shoes for the most part) and never seemed to bathe. From their smell you can hardly tell them from the sheep, what with the rough tunic and wooly skin coats they wear about their shoulders. He realized it was all they had to protect themselves from the relentless heat of the sun during the day and to cover themselves at night to ward off the chilly wind blowing across the desert floor. Even the pointed little animal skin hats they wore made them look somewhat akin to the animals they tended.

Such a simple life these shepherds live, he thought. *Day in and day out their only concern is to protect their sheep from predators.* Of course, protecting those flocks from hyenas, foxes, wild dogs, an occasional lion, and sometimes marauding nomads was important. But compared with the life of an up-and-coming young Roman soldier like himself, Artie could not help but think he could never spend his life leading a flock of smelly sheep to green pastures in the springtime, then hoping to find a patch of dried-up grass to sustain life in the summer and late fall before heading back to the fold in the winter months. And there was the never-ending search for water to quench the thirst of both animals and men. Without a constant source of water to sustain life, the desert was unforgiving for both man and beast.

Snapping out of that line of thought, Artie realized how much he liked a well-prepared meal of lamb in the local Jewish eateries, and the warm clothing his government provided Roman soldiers made from sheep's wool. *Without those simple shepherds,* he thought, *who would care for the bleating beasts?* In addition to the meat and wool they provided, he also had heard that special flocks were raised for certain Jewish religious ceremonies as "sacrificial sheep," something about "an atonement for sins committed." *These religious practices of the Jews certainly were strange.*

Lost in his thoughts, Artie had nearly forgotten the two Jewish servants walking with him. But his ears perked up when he heard them discussing a group known as "The Way" and particularly a prominent member of this group named Simon Peter. That man had stirred up a ruckus in Jerusalem some time ago when he and a few other men founded a new religion of sorts following the death of their leader, a man from Nazareth in Galilee.[1]

They referred to their leader as *Yeshua*, who claimed to be the Jewish *Messiah*. This outraged the chief priests of the temple, who considered the man to be just a common carpenter and stonemason who surrounded himself with a rag-tag group of uneducated men. *Yeshua* further angered the Jewish leadership by traveling around the countryside, announcing that the kingdom of heaven was at hand. At their insistence, they had *Yeshua* arrested, tried for crimes against both Rome and the Jewish nation, and put to death on a cross by the Roman government.

This same Peter was said to have spoken at an event in Jerusalem which drew several thousand people, and where he and several of his friends supposedly spoke in many different languages simultaneously about this new religion. Furthermore, Peter had said that peculiarity had been predicted hundreds of years earlier by one of their esteemed Jewish prophets.[2] *If this is the man Cornelius has sent me to bring back from Joppa, I can't help but wonder what it would be like to meet him in person*, Artie pondered.

His mind then returned to Cornelius himself. *What has happened to him? Is he becoming religious? How can a centurion, entrusted with an important garrison like Caesarea, be so taken in by the domain of mystics and aesthetics? Did he actually see an angel, or was he overcome by the heat of the day, perhaps had too much wine, or is it his older age kicking in? Do angels even exist?* Artie was deeply troubled by such thoughts. Throughout his life he had heard of many religions, and as a small boy taught emperor worship. Was not Caesar the only god he ever needed to serve?

Artie felt that Cornelius had become somewhat confused regarding angels, but deep inside he sensed something just was not right concerning his own philosophy about religion. He felt there might be something more required to give a man greater moral strength, peace of mind, and quietness of heart. He had hoped this could be accomplished by trying to emulate his centurion. Now he was not so sure.

What were the thoughts of these two men traveling with him? He knew they too must have been told of the strange events their master had experienced yesterday. Being trusted family servants, they did not appear to be shocked by the news but instead seemed pleased their master had entrusted them with this journey. For his part, as a soldier of Rome, Articus would rather have made the trip alone. He could have made better time and, using the power of his office, have ordered the man to waste no time in going with him to Caesarea for an audience before an official representative of the emperor. While he thought it strange his centurion sent two simple servants along with him to fetch a Jewish upstart, he would have felt more strange had he realized Cornelius actually was relying more on those two believing servants than on this brash young warrior!

Finally, Artie interrupted his musings by turning to the men and asking, "Tell me something? Is your master really serious about religion? Do you think he really takes his prayers to heart and attempts to talk directly with a god or gods? If anyone knows your master's thinking it should be the two of you."

The taller of the two men cast a sideways glance at the Roman soldier but did not speak. As a long-time servant to the centurion, his expression was that of a man who long-ago had learned the value of keeping his master's business private. It was hard to read his face. He would, no doubt, make a worthy opponent at games of chance where one must not divulge a winning hand too quickly. The other man, somewhat shorter, thick-waisted, and built like a Spartan wrestler, seemed on the verge of delivering a speech every time he was asked a question on any subject. The sparkle in his eyes, crease lines of his smile, frown of his brow, and animated body language, spoke volumes. It was he who responded to the soldier's question.

"Our master is not an easy man to know. He is a study in contrasts. A powerful and influential man of the sword, he can command men in war and peace and does not hesitate to make hard choices in battle, even at the risk of loss of blood and life. At the same time, he is a gentle man who loves his family dearly, cares for the hardships and suffering of others, and has been known personally to attend the bedside of many of his men who lingered at death's door, dispatched there by the cruelties of war.

"He sent us to Joppa for good reason. As a man under the authority of Rome, our centurion understands well the system called "chain-of-command," where one's authority is based on being subject to a higher commander. He also believes that his vision yesterday came from the god of the Jews (*Yahweh*), and that the man in Joppa is *Yahweh's* servant, under the command of *Yahweh*. Our centurion recalled an instant when the young servant of one of his commanders was confined to bed, paralyzed and in great pain. Our master pleaded with *Yeshua*, also known as the "Healer," to come and heal him. When the Healer said he would, the commander said that was not necessary, that all *Yeshua* had to do was simply give the command and the servant would be healed. That was because the commander knew that to have authority one had to be under authority. So, *Yeshua* gave the word, and the servant was healed.³ If indeed our centurion's vision did come from *Yahweh*, then the man in Joppa who is under *Yahweh's* authority will be able to explain what the vision meant. That is why he has sent us there to bring him to Caesarea. Our task is to make his journey as safe and comfortable as possible."

At these words Artie stopped abruptly, staring intently at both men. The servants stopped as well, wondering if they were going to be scolded by their escort for having spoken out so boldly. But after a few silent moments, Artie resumed his walk, pondering in his heart the things he had seen and heard over the past two days.

Notes

1. Acts 2:5–13
2. Joel 2:28–29
3. Matthew 8:5–13

CHAPTER

7

THE VISION

He saw the sky open, and something like a large sheet was let down by its four corners. In the sheet were all sorts of animals, reptiles, and birds.

Acts 10:11–12

The sun had reached its zenith. A few wispy clouds drifted lazily off to the southwest like campfire smoke escaping the bonds of earth, slowly dissipating in an endless blue sky. It was one of those scorching days of summer where residents escaped to the roofs of their homes, hoping to catch any small breezes drifting along the coast of the great sea. On hot nights the roof often became one's sleeping quarters when such breezes could mean the difference between sleep and fitful wakefulness. Typically, rooftops in this part of the world served many useful purposes, including storage for flax and grain, dining and entertaining, and even as catch basins for rainwater to be channeled down into a home's cistern.

The more affluent citizens of Joppa built their houses high in the surrounding hills, where the breezes often were brisker and could be channeled through specially designed openings in the walls. But the home of Simon the Tanner was located down along the seashore, close to the waters of the Mediterranean Sea. Breezes here tended to be warm and humid, saturated with the sticky salty brine of the sea. But the waters were useful for the tanning process.

Simon Peter moved along the edge of the roof, seeking an optimum point from which to catch any cooling breezes. He drew in a deep breath of salty air, tinged with just a hint of the fishy aroma of the sea combined with the acrid smell of hides being tanned. A born fisherman, Peter's thoughts seldom strayed far from his passion for the trade. Even though he had been trained and commissioned to become "a fisher of men,"[1] even now he occasionally chose to spend a few days seaside, visiting his friend Simon, known by most as "Simon the Tanner."

Either by reputation or by their smell, tanners were not considered among the best friends to have. The process of tanning hides is smelly at best. At times it is almost unbearable due to the odiferous ingredients used in the process. Salt brine from the sea, animal dung, and other caustic mixtures are the main reason hides take on their color and supple texture. When combined with the natural properties of the animal skins, the final product has a moderated leathery smell but also leaves the tanner's hands and arms leathery and discolored and laced with the permanent pungent smell of the chemicals utilized in the process. It is the main reason many tanners do not marry and have families and is acceptable grounds for a legal divorce by a tanner's wife when she no longer can stand the odor.

Tanners' homes and businesses often were combined and usually located by a sea due to the need for large amounts of seawater that were drawn and placed in large vats. There the skins could be soaked and scrubbed for many days to produce the finished products. It also helped to have the constant sea breezes carrying away the acrid smell of the tanning chemicals. Such was the home where Peter had come to visit his friend Simon. Whether it was the smell of the salty sea air or the isolation from outsiders provided by the tanning odors, it was where this "Fisher of Men" sought a time of prayerful solitude. In those exhausting weeks after Pentecost when Peter and the other apostles introduced the new age of grace to thousands who believed, Peter needed the rest. He recalled how frequently *Yeshua* would withdraw by himself to a place of solitude to rest and pray[2] and felt the same need himself. Whatever the reason, at that moment Peter was up on Simon's rooftop and becoming very hungry!

An apostle and a member of the group known as "The Way," Peter always enjoyed the hospitality he found at Simon's home. Here he could relax and rest from his busy schedule of spreading the good news that *Messiah* had come. The pace of life in Joppa was much more subdued than in Jerusalem, where opposition from the Pharisees and others in the *Sanhedrin* was creating serious problems for those who belonged to "The Way." Even among those who believed that *Yeshua* was the long sought-after *Messiah*, there were some who were uncertain as to what degree members of this new faith should obey the Law of Moses. Peter also was unsure, but before many more days would elapse, he would find himself back in Jerusalem dealing with that issue. However, for now he was just looking forward to spending time in his friend's home praying, meditating, and seeing what the Spirit of the Lord might reveal to him from day-to-day.

Downstairs, a meal was being prepared. Between heavy odors of salty air and the tanning process, Peter caught brief whiffs of an inviting aroma, perhaps a curried lamb stew mixed with rich spices and fresh vegetables. The savory fragrance made him realize he was hungrier than he had first imagined, even to the extent it was hindering his prayers! He found his mind drifting back and forth between thoughts of satisfying his hunger to praising *Yahweh* for His love and bountiful blessings.

Suddenly Peter became aware of *Yahweh's* Holy Spirit revealing to him a strange and confusing sight. Whether in a trance or a vision he was not sure, but the azure skies seemed to part, making way for a heavenly revelation. An object like a large sheet slowly descended, supported by unseen restraints at its four corners. It was filled with all manner of four-footed beasts, reptiles, and even birds. As his mind struggled to grasp the meaning of such a sight, he heard a command from heaven saying to him, "*Arise, Peter, kill and eat!*"

Peter's immediate response was "Surely not Lord, for I have never eaten anything impure or unclean."

Again a voice came to him a second time, "What *Yahweh* has made clean, no longer consider unholy." This happened three times, and immediately the object was taken up into the sky.[3] Finally the sheet was taken back into the heavens, leaving Peter alone on the rooftop, shaken and puzzled by this strange occurrence.

Notes

1. Matthew 4:19
2. Matthew 14:23, Mark 1:35
3. Acts 10:9–16

CHAPTER

8

THE TANNER'S HOUSE

So he took him into his house and...washed their feet and they ate and drank.

Judges 19:21

"This must be the place," declared Artie, taking note of the small stone house in front of him. "At least it smells like it!" he muttered to himself. While gesturing to the two servants with him, he held his nose and said: "It smells like one of those barbarian warriors I fought during my first real battle as a fighter for Caesar." Making no attempt to disguise his contempt for the odor he went on: "I love the smell of leather, but I think the tanning process would offend even the noses of the gods." Thinking of the beautiful young woman he had seen in the marketplace at Caesarea, he wondered why any man in his right mind would become a tanner if it caused him to lose the love of a woman like her. Even without the smell, a sign on the property which said "Tanning Goods by Simon" told the travelers they had arrived.

The building in front of them was a weather-worn stone and rock structure, typical of homes found near the seashore. A never-ending mixture of wind, salt spray, and the blistering sun worked together to etch a unique bleached charm into the wooden shutters and doors of the modest dwelling.

A low, crooked stone fence rambled along the front of the dwelling, enclosing a small courtyard where two sickly palms and a couple of scrub bushes provided sparse shade from the blistering heat. The only furnishings in the courtyard were a rough wooden table and a couple of crude chairs, one a bit lopsided. A misshapen and bleached wooden gate, standing slightly ajar and somewhat askew due to a broken leather hinge, breached the stone fence. One was reminded of the saying that "a cobbler repairs all but his own shoes." In this case, the tanner had neglected his own leather-hinged gate.

Along one side of the stacked-stone dwelling, a crude staircase clung to the house and ascended to the top of the one-story structure. With no safety railing, one had to exercise caution climbing the stairs. However, as required by the Law of Moses, a low parapet ran along the roof line providing an element of safety from an accidental fall from the roof.[1] The stairs ended in a small opening for access to the flat roof. This type of dwelling was very common in that region and added extra room to the structure. There one could host guests or catch any breezes from the sea while relaxing under a makeshift straw covering designed to ward off the sun. Artie thought to himself, "How crude these people are in their home designs; certainly not like the grandeur of the homes of Rome!"

Being aware of how testy Jews were about letting a Gentile set foot on their property—and wanting to be as diplomatic as possible—he cleared his throat and most respectfully called out: "Salutation to the house of Simon the Tanner. I am a Roman soldier on official business seeking an audience with one Simon, known also as Peter. Is such a man staying here?"

Artie's call roused Peter from his deep thoughts concerning the vision he had just received from the Lord. God's Spirit assured him that the men down below had come in peace and meant him no harm. With that assurance, he immediately proceeded downstairs to greet them.[2]

"Are you the master of the house or the one known as Simon Peter?" inquired the young officer.

"I am Simon Peter, but why do you ask? What do you want?"

"I am Articus Quintus, a soldier of Rome under the command of Cornelius, Centurion of Caesarea. I bring a message from him with his request that you return with me and his servants for an audience before him. About this time yesterday he had a heavenly vision in which an angel directed him to send for a man called Simon Peter here in Joppa and at this house."[3]

Upon receiving this message, Peter conferred with Simon. As their host, the tanner welcomed the three strangers into his home, had a servant wash their feet, and invited them to share the meal that had been prepared. Mindful of the next day's return trip to Caesarea, they were grateful for the humble hospitality of Simon's home to rest after their long walk. That evening, Simon prepared sleeping accommodations on the rooftop for his guests, where he hoped night breezes would afford the best opportunities for sleeping.

After sending the travelers up to bed and wishing them God's rest and safety through the night, Peter had a serious discussion with Simon the tanner and several other friends. What was their advice concerning Peter's going with a Roman soldier and Cornelius's servants to the centurion's citadel in Caesarea? Could it be a trick of some kind to get Peter into the clutches of the Roman government, known for its desire to appease the Jewish leaders who were calling for the extermination of the new religion founded by *Yeshua*? In the time that had passed since His crucifixion, the number of His disciples and followers had increased so greatly that it had greatly increased friction between opposing factions of Jews, tensions which even had begun to register among Gentiles and the Roman military.

As each man spoke his opinion and fears, Peter listened intently. Would his going mean a complete disregard for his personal safety; would he symbolically be walking into a lions' den?[4] After all Cornelius, Centurion of Caesarea, was a high military official who affirmed total fidelity to Caesar, a man who claimed not only to be the god of Rome but also the entire known world. The men before Peter were deeply concerned that he might be walking blindly into a cleverly laid trap.

Finally, the apostle gestured for calm and quiet. After expressing great appreciation for their concerns and counsel, he told them of his experience on the rooftop earlier that afternoon where he had seen a vision of animals being let down from heaven in a sheet while a voice on high spoke saying "*Rise, Peter, kill and eat.*"

"Men," Peter continued, "I responded to that voice by saying, '*By no means Lord, for I have never eaten anything that is common or unclean.*' Then the voice came to me a second time saying, '*What Yahweh has made clean, do not call impure.*' After this happened three times, the sheet was taken back into heaven. Almost immediately, the *Spirit of Yahweh* told me three men even then were inquiring downstairs for me. The *Spirit* instructed me not to hesitate to meet them, as He had sent them to fetch me.[5]

"So, you see, men, I have no fear for what I am about to do. I will accompany these men from Caesarea and talk with this Roman centurion about whatever our Lord tells me to say. I believe the vision I had this afternoon indicates that I am to treat all men the same regarding their need to receive *Yeshua* as their Savior. *Yahweh* does not respect people regarding race, culture or the nation to which they belong.[6] All men need to be at peace with *Yahweh* by learning the truth about our Lord and *Messiah, Yeshua*, and be given the opportunity to receive Him."

This unexpected revelation that *Yahweh's Spirit* had communicated with Peter caused quite a stir among those present. However, it gave them better understanding as to why they could not dissuade Peter from going to meet with Cornelius. After a few moments of counsel among themselves they told Peter that even so, they felt compelled to accompany him on the journey to Caesarea. That being settled, the men joined in a season of prayer before all retired for the night, anticipating the long journey ahead.

Notes

1. Deuteronomy 22:8
2. Acts 10:19-20
3. Acts 10:56
4. Daniel 6:16-21
5. Acts 10:9-19
6. Acts 10:34

CHAPTER 9

SLEEPLESS IN JOPPA

"I lie awake, I have become like a lonely bird on a housetop."
Psalm 102:7

Artie studied the vast expanse of the night sky sparkling with embers of light glowing against a canvas of black. He could not remember seeing the heavens look so radiant. The stars, so brilliant and dazzling, seemed like diamonds or gemstones scattered as pinpoints of light on a sea of ink. It was indeed a king's feast for his eyes. The night sky was both vast and beautiful. A measure of heat given up by the sunbaked earth was tempered by a slight chill in the night air. A soft breeze was blowing in from the sea, and in the distance he could hear the gentle splashing of the surf as each wave coursed its way from sea to shore.

Artie treasured the night. It slowed the hustle and bustle of the day and gave one pause for reflection. Purple shadows of darkness covered the harshness of daily life. The scars, bruises, and injuries to men and buildings, mountains and valleys seemed less cruel. Yes, night could be a cover for those plotting evil or filled with anguish for the lonely, but it also served to slow the busyness of life's hectic pace and give rise to moments of solitary reflection. It was during those times of reflection when Artie felt empty, as though something was missing in his life. He deeply longed to hold a woman in his arms, to rest in her warmth and embrace, finding purpose in life through the stability of family, love, and little ones nestled nearby in the safety and security of their parents' protection.

The mat the tanner had provided was amply cushioned with plenty of straw but sleep eluded Artie. Lying flat on his back with fingers entwined behind his head, far too many thoughts crowded his mind, some being of the girl with beautiful eyes and smile he had met in the Caesarea market. Was that meeting a chance encounter or fate at work? He could not remember ever before feeling this way about a girl, especially one he'd just met. Who was she, where did she live, and what was she like? He still could remember the soft warm touch of her hand, her shy smile, and enchanting eyes. Out loud he said, "Quit kidding yourself!" But inwardly he hoped he might see her again, not knowing where or when.

Then his thoughts turned back to this strange mission on behalf of his centurion. What was it all about, and who was this man named Simon *but called Peter*? What information could he possibly have that was of such great importance to Cornelius?

As time passed it became evident that sleep had eluded him; so, Artie arose and slipped on his tunic and sandals. He quietly made his way down the outer stairs, across the courtyard, and out through the broken gate. A full moon stood watch high in the night sky, bathing the sleeping village in pale lunar light. Except for the occasional barking of a neighborhood dog, the night remained peaceful and still.

Cautiously making his way down to the shoreline, Artie paused for a few moments listening to the soft gentle motion of the incoming surf. The mesmerizing swish of each wave lapping at the shore soothed his mind and calmed his spirit. A sliver of moonbeam danced across the waters of the great sea, highlighting the fluorescence of the seafoam riding the crest of each wave. Artie removed his tunic and sandals, letting them fall on the soft warm sand. After a few hesitant steps into the surf, he quickly dove beneath the water, allowing its warmth to encase his body completely. Quickly he swam perhaps thirty yards toward the open sea, then did a rolling dive to reverse directions and swim once again toward the beach. As he emerged from the salty sea his body glistened with sea salt, and bits of sand clung to his arms, legs, and torso. The young soldier ran both hands through his hair scooping the water back toward his neck. He wiped the sea spray from his face, arms, and legs, then rubbed vigorously to allow the night air to dry his skin. Nearly dry, he picked up his sandals, tied them together and slung them over his left shoulder. Then he tied his short tunic around his waist, leaving the remainder of his body exposed to dry in the warm night air. Greatly refreshed and wide awake, he paused, scanned the shoreline in both directions, turned to his right, and began to walk slowly along the shore, allowing the warm waters of the sea to lap gently about his feet. The soothing waters warmed not only his feet but his heart as well. There was something about the tender embrace of the warm salty liquid that calmed his body, soul, and spirit, and brought a sense of deep relaxation to the young soldier. Artie took a long deep breath of sea air through his nostrils until his lungs were filled to capacity, then he slowly exhaled, relishing the energizing force. Just then a gentle breeze massaged his body. This exhilaration of his senses caused him to realize that he had a good life and much to be thankful for, so why sometimes during quiet private moments did he feel a sense of loneliness and a feeling that something was lacking in his life? It was as if a part of him was missing—a completeness that would give him purpose and direction. Here on this lonely stretch of shoreline—looking out toward the vastness of the sea, beneath the shimmering moonlight and the limitless scope of the heavens above—he felt so small and insignificant. With no family to speak of and not many close friends, all he had was his service to Rome and faith in his mentor, Cornelius. But Cornelius's sudden interest in religion and seeing a heavenly vision troubled Artie. Had he placed his faith in men who could change their minds and leave him not knowing what to believe?[1]

Suddenly his thoughts were broken by a slight noise behind him. Sensing he was not alone Artie turned quickly, pulse racing and body tense, muscles taut for a possible attack. Spotting a figure moving slowly in his direction, Artie reached for his dagger, realizing too late he had left his weapon back at the house.

"Halt, who goes there, friend or foe?"

"Fear not, it is only I, Marcus, humble servant to Centurion Cornelius. I mean you no harm." Indeed, it was Marcus, the shorter of the two servants who had traveled with Articus to Joppa, the one whose face betrayed his moods so easily.

After putting his clothes back on, Artie allowed him to approach a few more feet before speaking again. "Are you following me Marcus? Has sleep escaped you on this strange mission, or do you want to tell me something?"

"I guess I'm too tired to sleep. Many thoughts have crowded sleep from my mind tonight. My mind particularly is drawn to the visitation by the angel of God my master experienced. Are you curious about that too?"

Artie did not reply but turned and resumed his walk along the beach while contemplating Marcus's question. Presuming that silence gives consent, Marcus quickly moved to Artie's side, and for the next few minutes they simply walked together without talking. Finally, Artie broke the silence.

"Tell me about your master. What kind of a man is he; have you served him long?"

"I have not. Until a few years ago I served under another centurion, a good man who treated me well and found favor with many men in Capernaum, the city where he had been assigned by Rome."

"So how did you come to work for Centurion Cornelius?"

"My first master died, killed in a street brawl by radical elements of Capernaum who sought to overthrow Roman occupation. Some say it was an accident when a large, loose stone fell from the top of a building while my master was trying to reason with two sides embroiled in the controversy. But I believe it was intentional. The stone struck with such force on his left shoulder and neck that my master sustained critical injuries. He was taken to his bed where he lingered several days, attended by his good friend and fellow centurion, Cornelius, who stayed by his side until he died. From his deathbed my master implored Cornelius to take me as his own servant and to treat me well for his sake. He was a good man, and I miss him greatly. But I find that Cornelius is much like my former centurion, especially in his attention to religious matters."

"What do you mean?" asked Artie, as he interrupted their stroll and turned to face the servant?

"As I said, my former master was a good man. He really cared for me, not just as a servant but as another human being. I never understood how much he cared until the time I fell desperately sick with an unknown illness. At first, I just experienced a little fever and minor achiness throughout my body. However, within a short time I was confined to my bed with delirium, not knowing whether it was day or night and unable to control my arms or legs. Death hung over me like the Sword of Damocles.[2] For a long time my mind drifted in a fog of delirium until I suddenly awoke as from a long restful sleep, fully refreshed and ready to meet the challenges of a new day. Not a sign of the illness lingered. I felt rested and well, as if I had never encountered so close a brush with death.

"Immediately after my remarkable recovery my master came to my bedside. He did not seem at all shocked or surprised to see me sitting up, in my right mind and fully healed of the strange malady that had appeared to be my death sentence. He told me a story that to this day I still find quite unbelievable and a bit strange. It involved his encounter with a Jewish man whom some say is the *Messiah* of the Jews."

"Master said when he saw the state I was in, out of my head, paralyzed, and suffering terribly, he was compelled to do something. He had become aware there was a recent arrival to the city named *Yeshua* who many proclaimed to be a mighty man of God. *Yeshua* was said to be able to heal the sick, produce miracles from God, and even raise the dead. My centurion immediately sought him out and begged him to heal me. This healer agreed to come at once and attend to me in my distress.

"My master then said he did not deserve to have him come to his house, but to just *"say the word and my servant will be healed*.' As a well-trained commanding officer who greatly respected the chain-of-command he also said: '*I too am a man under authority, with soldiers under me; and I say to this one, 'Go!' and he goes, and to another, 'Come!' and he comes, and to my slave, 'Do this!' and he does it.*" Then *Yeshua* said to my master, "*Go, it shall be done for you as you have believed.*" Marcus paused for a minute before saying, " *And I was healed that very moment.*"[3] Then he lowered his head, and began watching a small wave—its energy spent—start to recede from the shore, dragging bits of sand and shells back toward the restless waters of the sea. As it did, the sandy soil churned until it partially buried both men's feet.

Artie stood for a moment watching the servant's meditation until he no longer could stand it: "Well, did anything else happen?"

Raising his head slowly and looking intently at Artie the servant spoke again: "This is the strange part. Master said that *Yeshua* seemed astonished that a Roman officer, a Gentile, accepted him so easily and said to the crowd around him, '*I tell you the truth, I have not found anyone in Israel with such great faith.*"[4] Unable to hold back any longer, Artie blurted out: "What did *Yeshua* mean when he said, '*Go; it will be done as you have believed it would*?'"

Before replying, Marcus cast a pensive gaze toward the distant horizon. The night breeze had picked up a bit and began tousling the dark locks of the servant's hair. Attempting to be more serious and composed, he ran his fingers unconsciously through his thick mane seeking with little success to comb it back into place. Then, drawing a deep breath, he finally spoke.

"My centurion told me he went to the Healer believing that I would be healed. And the very hour *Yeshua* spoke those words, the sickness left my body. That fact was confirmed by the other household servants, but I, myself, cannot say what happened. However, I know my illness departed very suddenly at a time when others felt my future in this life was grim.

"Master gave credit to *Yeshua* and said that he indeed must be more than a mere man. From that day until his untimely death several weeks later, my master was a different person. At times he was almost fanatical in his belief that he had found the true path to *Yahweh*. He constantly spoke of a personal relationship with the God of the whole universe. He even felt that to know *Yeshua* was to know *Yahweh*.

"Along with other members of the household, I feared for my former master's right mind. Yet, we saw a peace and calm about him that drew us to want to know more about what he had come to possess. I found myself asking him many questions about this new life he was experiencing, but before I could ask all my questions, he died. In the confusion, fear, anger, and sadness that surrounded our master's death, I was much too caught up in what was going on in this life to dwell much on matters of the next life. My greatest fear was that I would be sold to a new owner who would be a harsh taskmaster, but my fears were unfounded. Complying with my dead master's wish, Cornelius became my new master. I soon found he is like my former master, a good man who cares not only for his immediate family, but also his servants and all those who are under his command.

"He is a religious man, and I often find him alone on his knees praying to his god. It is only in the past few months that he has shared with me intimate thoughts about his own life, death, and things concerning the possible existence of only one god. Like you, I am puzzled concerning this journey he has sent us on and in the events that preceded it. I too am curious as to what light this fisherman can shed on the strange visitation Cornelius had."

At this juncture, Marcus hesitated so long that Artie prompted: "I sense you want to tell me something more, what is it?"

"There is another reason I followed you tonight, one which might shed more light on why we have been tasked with bringing Simon Peter back to Caesarea.

"After our evening meal, I was talking with several men here at the Tanner's house who are curious about our visit. They told me something that I think you will find of interest. They think perhaps that what they told me may have come to the attention of our centurion and be a major reason he wants to meet him.

"It seems that shortly after Simon Peter arrived here to visit with the tanner, he was told of the death of a woman named Tabitha, also known as Dorcas. Evidently, she was popular and well thought of among the widows of this region and may have been a widow herself. She was known as an excellent seamstress, making beautiful clothes and robes for others. She was a follower of *Yeshua* and belonged to the local group known as "The Way." Immediately, Peter went to the home where Tabitha's body was laid out in preparation for burial. There he found many ladies wailing and moaning over Tabitha's death, trying all at once to show many of the clothing items she had made. Personally, I wonder if they were grieving as much because she wouldn't be making any more clothes for them as it was for the fact she had died!

"They told me he sent all the ladies out of the room, shut the door, got down on his knees next to the body, and began to pray. Then in a loud voice he told her to get up! With that '… *she opened her eyes, and when she saw him, she sat up. And he gave her his hand and raised her up; and calling in the other widows, he presented her alive.*' News of this event spread all over Joppa and in nearby cities. Because of it, many more people here have become followers of 'The Way.'"[5]

Marcus continued: "Through the remarkable recovery from my own illness, I personally have experienced the healing power of *Yeshua*. From what I learned this evening about the fisherman, it appears *Yeshua's* power has been passed on to a few men he taught personally who are called 'apostles.' If that is true, I really would like to meet the man who raised Dorcas back to life; it certainly is powerful enough reason for Cornelius to want to meet him in person."

Notes

1. Psalm 118:8–9
2. The famed Sword of Damocles dates back to an ancient moral parable popularized by the Roman philosopher Cicero in his 45 B.C. book, *Tusculan Disputations*.
3. Matthew 8:5–13
4. Luke 7:1–9
5. Acts 9:36–41

CHAPTER
10

PETER & ARTICUS

Three men appeared at the house in which we were staying, having been sent to me from Caesarea. The Spirit told me to go with them without misgivings.

Acts 11:11–12

Streaks of gold graced the horizon as if painted by the broad strokes of a painter's brush, causing the darkness slowly to give way to the promise of another beautiful day. The two servants who had come with Artie, together with Peter and his friends, had begun the return trip to Caesarea along the same hot dusty road they had traveled just the day before. The difference now was in their direction of travel and the number in their party. Simon Peter had prevailed upon six of his friends to make the journey with him.[1]

What surprised Artie was their willingness to set aside other plans to accompany Peter to a meeting with a Roman centurion, not knowing its real purpose or potential outcome. Were they concerned that Peter was in danger of being charged with a crime against Rome, or was it an attempt to disrupt his extraordinary ministry in Joppa? Did they think their presence might provide a favorable witness for Peter against any false accusations? Whatever their reason, Artie couldn't help but admire their commitment to give moral support to this itinerant fisherman. None of the small party traveling back to

Caesarea could have foreseen the historic impact coming out of this meeting of diverse nationalities and cultures.

Artie was not alone in his musing. For as they walked, Peter continued to ponder the meaning of his vision of unclean animals being let down in a sheet, wondering as to the full extent of its significance. Did the animals represent a change in the Lord's commands concerning unclean animals,[2] or did it have more to do with relationships between Jews and Gentiles? Exactly what was the *Spirit of the Lord* trying to tell him with such a strange vision, and how did it relate to his forthcoming meeting with the Roman centurion? So many questions were swirling around in Peter's mind!

He then turned his thoughts to the young Roman soldier escorting the group to Caesarea. Since his youth, Peter had despised the foreigners who occupied his homeland. But three years spent with *Yeshua* had changed his heart. Now he couldn't help but feel a sense of compassion for the young soldier, serving far from home in a country where most, as Peter had previously, resented his very presence.

The powerful Roman army had swept through the promised land like a plague of locusts and, with the aid of superior weapons, quickly took control of Jerusalem and God's people. As a boy he often had heard the elders bemoan that Israel was conquered as punishment for its sins against Jehovah God. However, they said there would come a day when the Lord would restore Israel to her rightful place in the world. As a youth Peter had embraced this hope and aligned himself with the Zealot movement,[3] which sought to force the issue of a free Israel restored to her past glory. He had longed for the day when the occupiers would leave, and the *Sanhedrin* once again would rule righteously over Israel with a strong core of elders.

Then the temple would regain its glory and grandeur as a beacon of light, honoring *Yahweh*. This was his thinking and zeal before he met *Yeshua*.

As if it were only yesterday, Peter remembered very well his first few encounters with the *Messiah*. The great teacher who seemed to have so much personal knowledge of Holy Writ and had such great passion in his delivery was the talk of all Palestine. Several times as he heard *Yeshua* speak, Peter strangely was drawn to him and his words. With nearly everyone he spoke to back then, Peter couldn't stop talking about him and his teachings, and he couldn't help but wonder, "Is this the anointed leader who will free Israel from her bondage?" If he was, Peter as a Zealot had been ready to follow him as the strong leader who would restore Israel to her past glory. But his encounters with *Yeshua* changed all that. Strong leadership alone was insufficient for a man with Peter's driving force and impetuous nature.

There came a day when he and his brother Andrew were hard at work, plying their nets in the waters of the Galilee hoping for a bountiful catch. The day began like a thousand others, perhaps a bit cooler than normal but not a cloud in the sky. After the usual preparation of getting their boat and fishing gear ready, they pushed out from shore and spread their nets in expectation of a good catch. Back on shore they could see their friends, fellow commercial fishermen James and John, with their father Zebedee and a hired man. All four were sitting in their boat mending nets broken from yesterday's bountiful haul. The waters of the sea were calm and silky smooth, with the sound of waves punctuated by a scattering of seabirds circling overhead, noisily making known their desire for a few morsels of fish or other tidbits tossed out for them to fight over.

While carefully watching his nets and trying to keep his balance when the boat was rocked by larger waves, someone on shore caught his eye. Even at a distance, Peter knew instinctively it was *Yeshua*—and he was looking straight at Peter and Andrew. With a mesmerizing look the teacher shouted to the two brothers, " *'Follow Me, and I will make you fishers of men.' Immediately they left their nets and followed Him.*"[4] On that fateful day, little did Peter know what it would mean to become "a fisher of men." Within a short time, *Yeshua* also invited brothers James and John to join him. Now, several years later, Peter understood more fully what a life-changing experience *Yeshua's* invitation had been for him.

Suddenly, Peter began to connect yesterday's vision with the reason he was going to Caesarea. Could it possibly be the Lord was telling him the message of salvation was not just for the Jews but for all men? Was God saying that *Yeshua* had died for all mankind, regardless of race, creed or color? Perhaps the young Roman soldier escorting them might give Peter an opportunity to see how that Gentile would react to the truth of *Yeshua's* words.

At noon the travelers stopped for a bite to eat near a small well surrounded by a grove of tall cedars. There, Peter left the rest of the party and drifted over to where Artie sat by himself, ever the protective military guard in a position where he could keep an eye on both those under his charge and the road itself. One never knew when highwaymen might be afoot!

"May I join you?" asked Peter.

"If you wish," replied Artie.

"I have the feeling you are none too happy with this assignment and that you'd prefer to be doing something other than this. To be perfectly honest, I too had not planned to be traveling today down a dusty road to Caesarea escorted by a Roman soldier. May I tell you about a great and wonderful happening in Jerusalem some time ago? I think it may give you a better understanding of who I am and why I now find myself as one of the leaders in the movement people call 'The Way.'" After Artie's grudging agreement, Peter continued.

"It was during Pentecost,[5] about seven weeks after *Yeshua* had been crucified, and devout Jews had come to Jerusalem representing nearly twenty nations, like Parthians, Medes, Cretans, Arabs, and more. Those of us who were Yeshua's close companions during his ministry were all together in a room worshiping and praying. Suddenly, a noise like a mighty wind erupted as if from heaven, and what appeared to be tongues of fire filled the place, then separated and came to rest on each of us. It was the Holy Spirit of *Yahweh* Himself! When those outside heard the noise, they came rushing into the house to see what it was all about. Then another miraculous event took place. Through the power of the *Holy Spirit*, we began speaking in such a way that each person present heard the message in their own language, even though all of us were speaking in *Aramaic*. It was a startling experience for everyone present. Some even accused us of being drunk, though it was only nine o'clock in the morning.

"It was then I felt the full impact of what *Yeshua* had told us about the *Holy Spirit* not long before He went to the cross. He had said He (*Yeshua*) would send the *Holy Spirit* to teach us and guide us into all truth[6] and bring to our minds[7] what we should say. Immediately I recalled the words of our Prophet Joel who had said: '*In the last days I will pour forth of My Spirit on all mankind; and your sons and your daughters shall prophesy, and your young men shall see visions, and your old men shall dream dreams.'*[8] I knew what we were experiencing was in partial fulfillment of that prophesy.

"Then, being emboldened by the *Holy Spirit,* I spoke with a loud voice on behalf of all eleven of us, for we stood together united. I explained to the listeners that we were not drunk, that what was happening had been prophesied, and by patient teaching that the man they had crucified was the promised *Messiah. Yahweh* had sent Him in the flesh to be born of a virgin and experience all the joys and travails of us human beings, then to die on the cross in His human form to be a sacrifice for the sins of all mankind, from the first to the last. In that manner *Yeshua* would reconcile sinful man to holy *Yahweh,* thus giving everlasting life in heaven to all who repented of their sins and received *Yeshua* as their kinsman-redeemer.[9]

"Many that day were convicted of their sins and exclaimed, 'What shall we do?' I declared to all: 'Repent and be baptized in the name of *Yeshua* for the forgiveness of your sins, and you also will receive the gift of the *Holy Spirit.*'[10] Artie, there were about three thousand people there that day who received *Yeshua* as their Lord and Savior and were baptized in His Name. Before that I believed salvation was only for the Jews, but *Yahweh* has shown me that all men, regardless of race or nation, can have everlasting life by receiving *Yeshua.*"

After hearing Peter's incredible story, Artie was at a loss for words. Either the man was out of his mind or a terribly inventive storyteller. Finally, he said to Peter, "If what you say is true, that *Yeshua* was the Son of *Yahweh,* then why was he crucified?

And what about the stories I've heard that he wanted to overthrow Roman rule and set up his own kingdom?"

In response Peter said: "*Yeshua* was crucified by Rome at the insistence of corrupt Jewish leaders. But you are mistaken my young friend if you think *Yeshua* spoke against Rome or was seeking to build a kingdom here on this earth. The kingdom he spoke of is a heavenly kingdom where his subjects will live for all eternity in peace and joy, enjoying fellowship with him such as never will be known on this earth. He never spoke against Rome, not one time. In fact, when asked about paying taxes he said: '*Render unto Caesar that which is Caesar's and to God that which is God's.*'[11] Those asking the question were troublemakers who hated him and wanted to trap him into speaking out against Caesar and Rome, but he refused to let them draw him into their web of lies and deceit."[12]

Stalling for time while trying to reconcile what he'd heard in the past with what this strange Jew was saying now, Artie broke off another piece of bread and popped it in his mouth. He chewed a moment, swallowed, and then took a drink from his wineskin. Rising to his feet he said: "As for my opinion about a Jewish carpenter dying and coming back to life, his being the Hebrew *Messiah* and there being a heavenly kingdom, that is far different than what I have been taught ... and it doesn't make any sense to me. For right now I'm simply carrying out my orders. Once we get to Caesarea, I'm certain we'll both learn more as to why my master felt it was so important for you to come and with such haste."

In both Roman and Jewish cultures, it was considered proper for a younger man to respect his elders, but Peter deferred to Artie as a representative of Rome. After receiving consent to talk further, Peter asked if he could address the young solder by his given name, Articus. Respectfully, Artie said, "Yes."

Peter then said: "It is my understanding that as a Roman soldier you are charged with keeping the peace here in Judea and throughout the Roman Empire. Rome proudly proclaims that once all the world is under the peace and justice of Rome, the system of justice administered under that rule will provide people everywhere with joy and happiness in life, knowing they are under the protection of Rome. Is that your understanding?"

Artie nodded his assent but said nothing.

"Well, Articus, as much as I might like to agree with that premise, I respectfully disagree. I believe true joy can never come to an individual because of peace, safety, justice, wealth, class distinction, or anything else. Real joy is an internal feeling of great pleasure or happiness that can come only by recognizing who *Yahweh* is, being guided by the Spirit of *Yahweh* to become more like Him, and living a life measured by letting *Yahweh* live through you. Articus, that's what real lasting joy and peace is; everything else is just ever-changing emotions based on constantly changing circumstances."

Not knowing how to respond, Artie stared at Peter for a long while, the silence broken only by the distant conversation of the others and the haunting song of a bird perched high in a tree. Looking up and seeing that it was yellow he wondered: "Is it the same one I heard back at the barracks or another like it? Its melody sounds the same." Seeking distraction, he turned his attention to a mongrel dog attracted by the smell of food. All skin and bones with tail tucked between his legs, the animal's head drooped down in submission. In some ways the dog was a picture of Artie himself. Alone without family in a strange country, wondering about the meaning of life and where to find truth, Artie wondered if the spiritual food he'd been given in the past was true meat or only scraps. Then he tossed the dog a scrap of bread and turned his attention back to Peter. "You have given me a greater understanding of your beliefs, sir, for which I am most appreciative. But at this point I cannot accept what you have told me."

Notes

1. Acts 11:12
2. Leviticus Chapter 11
3. As noted by the Jewish historian, Josephus, the Zealots were one of four First Century Jewish sects which included the Pharisees, Sadducees, and Essenes.
4. Matthew 4:19–20; Mark 1:16
5. Refers to the festival celebrated on the 50th day after Passover, also called "The Festival of Weeks."
6. John 16:12–13
7. John 14:26
8. Joel 2:28
9. Leviticus 25:47–55
10. Acts 2:1–41
11. Mark 12:17
12. Matthew 22:15–22; Mark 12:13–17

CHAPTER
11

THE HOUSE OF CORNELIUS

Blessed is the one who comes in the name of the LORD*;*
We have blessed you from the house of the LORD*.*

Psalm 118:26

The journey from Joppa to Caesarea followed the great road between Tyre and Egypt. After his conversation with Peter, Artie maintained his distance from the man and was relieved when he saw the gates of Caesarea looming in the distance. Built by Herod the Great, this beautiful city had been the official residence of the Herodian kings—Porcius Festus, Felix, and other Roman procurators of Judea. Not only did the city contain many magnificent buildings, but it also had a splendid harbor built at great cost. Unlike towns that the Jews had built, those erected by the Greeks and Romans tended to be well planned with wide paved streets. Squares were formed where major streets crossed one another, and there were many open areas in front of public buildings. Caesarea had a main street with shops on either side, plus splendid baths[1] and theaters. Houses were built in blocks of four, and there were many administrative buildings and places of entertainment. Though the town was a first-rate duty assignment for senior officers of Rome, Artie would have preferred an assignment back in Rome itself.

As they neared Cornelius' house, Artie wondered what the centurion would think of Peter's decision to bring along his friends. *Can you imagine his gall?* he asked himself. *Who in their right mind would bring along an entire entourage of six other loathsome Hebrews?* As a well-disciplined soldier, Artie would never have done such a thing himself! However, he needn't have been concerned, for Cornelius seemed delighted to see this band of men from Joppa. In fact, he seemed more excited than Artie ever before had seen him! Even more so, in anticipation of the arrival of Simon Peter, Cornelius had ordered that the house be set in order as though he were receiving a special dignitary from Rome herself. Not only that, but he had also called together many of his relatives and close friends.

To Artie's great shock, when Peter entered, Cornelius met him, fell at his feet, and worshiped him! To see the highest Roman authority in the region on his knees before a hated Hebrew was almost too much for Artie to take. "Had the centurion lost his mind? Why would he bow before a common Hebrew fisherman who never had commanded men in battle or led a nation to victory against foreign foes?" Then something even more unforgivable occurred! Peter took Cornelius by the hand and said: "*Stand up; I too am just a man.*" The fisherman continued: "*You yourselves know how unlawful it is for a man who is a Jew to associate with a foreigner or to visit him; and yet God has shown me that I should not call any man unholy or unclean. That is why I came with your men without even raising an objection. So, I ask, for what reason did you send for me?*"[2] Peter's statement about not calling any man "unholy or unclean" sent another shock wave through Artie. How could this unwashed fisherman call his centurion "unholy or unclean?" Surely it was a penalty worthy of death. Artie was so unnerved by it all that he wished he could just "evaporate" and be gone from the scene. How could he have placed so much devotion and hero-worship in Cornelius and then see him kneeling before the fisherman like a conquered slave?

In response, Cornelius told Peter about the vision he had received, and how specifically he had been instructed to call for a man named "Peter" who was staying in Joppa. Now that Peter was there, he and his household were waiting expectantly to hear all that God had given him to tell them.

The room fell silent as every ear and eye focused on the fisherman from Joppa. What would he have to say? Even Artie felt riveted to the spot where he stood. As much as he wanted to be elsewhere, something deep within him created a longing in his heart to hear what Peter would say. As though his sandals were fastened to the floor—and because of his sense of loyalty to his superior—he remained rooted in place.

Notes

1. Bath houses were centers not only for bathing but also socializing and reading as well. They were supplied with water from an adjacent river or stream or within cities by aqueducts. The water would be heated by fire then channeled into the caldarium (hot bathing room).
2. Acts 10:24–29

CHAPTER
12

THE MESSAGE

"How then will they call on Him in whom they have not believed? How will they believe in Him whom they have not heard? And how will they hear without a preacher? How will they preach unless they are sent? Just as it is written, 'HOW BEAUTIFUL ARE THE FEET OF THOSE WHO BRING GOOD NEWS OF GOOD THINGS!'"

Romans 10:14–15

Peter asked that everyone be seated, and for a few moments quietly surveyed his audience, making direct eye contact with each person in the room. He had a commanding presence about him that reminded Artie of high-ranking officers he had observed. Peter was obviously a man who was no pushover. He was a big man with the weatherworn appearance Artie had found so common among Jewish fishermen. With his rough-hewn looks, muscular build and "take charge" personality, he looked like he could handle himself well in a good street fight. His demeanor exuded the qualities Artie would expect from a Roman military commander he would follow into battle—a true "man's man!"

Peter bowed his head, closed his eyes, and for a few moments stood silent, with just a hint of perceivable movement from his lips.

What is he doing now? thought Artie. *Is he thinking about what to say, or perhaps praying to his god?*

Peter slowly raised his head, took a deep breath, and with a slight smile looked once more into the faces of each person in the room. When his eyes met those of Artie, he paused an extra moment or two as if he were studying deeply the innermost thoughts of the young officer. Finally, he began to speak.

"I have come to realize how true it is that *Yahweh* does not show favoritism to any but accepts men from every nation who fear him and do what is right.[1]

"Some of you here today know the message *Yahweh* has given to the people of Israel, telling the good news of peace through *Yeshua*, the *Messiah*, who is Lord of all.

"You know what happened throughout Judea, beginning in Galilee after the baptism that John the Baptist preached. How *Yahweh* anointed *Yeshua* with the *Holy Spirit* and power, and how He went about doing good and healing all who were under the power of the devil. He could do this because *Yahweh* was with Him.

"I and many others are personal witnesses of everything He did in Jerusalem and throughout Israel. Even so, the Jewish hierarchy incited my fellow countrymen to riot, demanding His death at the hands of the Roman authorities.[2] They killed Him by hanging Him on a tree, but *Yahweh* raised Him from the dead on the third day and many of us saw him alive after that. *Yeshua* was not seen by all the people, but by more than five hundred witnesses whom *Yahweh* had chosen, including those of us who ate and drank with Him after He rose from the dead.[3]

"Before He ascended into heaven, He met with us on a mountain in Galilee[4] where He gave us these instructions:

'All authority has been given Me in heaven and on earth. Go therefore and make disciples of all the nations, baptizing them in the name of the Father and the Son and the Holy Spirit, teaching them to observe all that I commanded you; and lo, I am with you always, even to the end of the age.'[5] By telling us to *'make disciples of all the nations'* He made it clear that Gentiles as well as Jews were invited to have a relationship with *Yahweh* the Father through *Yeshua*. In the process *Yahweh* adopts us into His family to become His children![6] Furthermore, we are to warn people there will come a time when all people will have to give account for how they lived their lives on this earth, and He will judge both the living and the dead.[7] But all who believe in *Yeshua* need not fear neither death nor His judgment for they already have received forgiveness of sins by accepting *Yeshua* as their Savior.'"[8]

Artie was listening so intently to Peter's message that he did not notice a disturbance in the room. First one individual and then another began to praise this Jewish God. As astonishing as such praise was, they seemed to be speaking in a variety of languages Artie did not recognize, perhaps like what one might hear in a bazaar frequented by merchants from various lands and cultures. While Artie was puzzled by what he saw and heard, Peter's six Jewish friends seemed even more surprised that the *Holy Spirit* had fallen upon Gentiles as well as on Jewish believers.[9]

Amidst the babble and general confusion, Artie felt he had seen and heard enough. In his mind it was hard not to compare those present with folks he had seen in the hands of a hypnotist or someone deluded by a medium. Worst of all he was fearful that his centurion was in danger of being swayed by

Peter's charisma into becoming a member of the impassioned group called "The Way." Unable to cope with anymore, he began to make his way to the door. Though he tried not to attract attention or cause a disturbance as he left, both Cornelius and his servant, Marcus, were very much aware of his departure.

Notes

1. Galatians 2:6
2. Mark 15:1–15; Luke 23:1–25; John 19:1–15
3. There are at least 10 references in the *New Testament* which attest to that fact. We have chosen two: to the 11 disciples in the upper room (Mark 16:14–18); and *"to more than 500"* in 1 Corinthians 15:6.
4. Though the name of this mountain is not identified in the *Bible*, it is generally thought to be MT Tabor.
5. Matthew 28:18–20
6. Ephesians 1:5
7. 1 Peter 4:5
8. Acts 10:34–43
9. Acts 10:44–46

CHAPTER
13

CENTURION'S PEACE OF HEART

*"You shall know the truth,
and the truth shall set you free."*
John 8:32

When Cornelius saw Artie slip out of the room, he felt for a moment the need to go after him. But he sensed the young man already was confused by the events of the past few days and knew the events of the meeting must have troubled him even more. To compound the situation, what might this zealous young soldier think if he suspected his commanding officer was replacing his allegiance to Rome with allegiance to the strange god of which Peter spoke? Cornelius made a mental note to talk with Artie as soon as possible, not just concerning the events of the past few days but as to why he had pulled strings to have Artie put under his command. Sharing that news with the young soldier also would give Cornelius the opportunity to tell him about the event that had awakened him to begin a personal search for the meaning of life. However, for now his mind was focused on what Peter was saying, for his words gave him a peace he'd never known until then.

In both heart and mind, Cornelius sensed that Peter's words were of truth, hope, and comfort. A flood of emotions filled his heart. It was as if a cool drink of water suddenly had filled every parched inch of his body. Was this feeling in his heart what they talked about as being *Yahweh's* love? As that sense of relief and calm came upon Cornelius, his anxiety about what it would take to please God was replaced by learning that *Yeshua* already had paid the price for all his sins and misdeeds. By accepting the *Good News of Yeshua*, he would become a child of *Yahweh*. What an awesome feeling both to know he didn't need do anything more than that, or to fear that whatever he did to earn *Yahweh's* favor could never be good enough. From his study of the Jewish religion and culture, Cornelius had learned that only the Jews had a covenant relationship with God.[1] Now Peter had said that he, a non-Jew, also could claim *Yahweh* as his Father. If this was so, it was as though he would be "born again"[2] as a son of *The Most High* in heaven! He now understood what others meant when they spoke of "The Way" as being about a relationship, not about religion. All of this was possible because *Yeshua* had died for the sins of all mankind, and he, Cornelius, now was trusting that fact for his salvation. In losing his own fears, Cornelius fully understood what he had seen in Marcus and in the good friend who had died in his arms: *Yeshua* truly had come from *Yahweh* in Heaven to take away the anguish, fear, sorrow, guilt, shame, and hurt of all who would invite Him into their lives.

As Cornelius and those of his household rejoiced at hearing the message of salvation, Peter's six Jewish friends didn't know what to think. Was it possible *Yahweh* was willing to accept these uncircumcised Gentiles into His kingdom even though they knew nothing of the Law and Commandments?

What about the giving of the *Holy Spirit*? The scene in the room made them think of Peter's message on the Day of Pentecost when the *Holy Spirit* came in like a rushing wind and all the apostles began speaking in other languages.[3] Indeed, Cornelius and those of his household were heard praising God and speaking in many different languages.[4]

Sensing the confusion on the faces of his friends, Peter turned his attention to them and spoke: "Can any of us keep these people from being baptized? As you can see, my brothers, they have received the *Holy Spirit* just as we have. It is *Yahweh's* desire that all people be part of His family and not perish[5] if they will accept the sacrifice made by *Yeshua's* death in payment for their sins. I understand this great truth even more now than I did at Pentecost. On Simon's rooftop in Joppa, an Angel sent by *Yahweh* showed me that all men everywhere can come to Him. Who are we to keep these who want to repent of their sins from doing so? If they believe in their hearts and confess with their mouths that *Yeshua* is Lord,[6] why should we stand in the way of their salvation?" Then Peter ordered that all who had made that decision were to be baptized.[7]

After those present who wanted to be baptized were, and the crowd thinned out, Cornelius made preparations for Peter and his friends to stay as his guests for a few days. The meeting had offered greater purpose to the vision *Yahweh* had given him to send for Peter, and now Cornelius was a happy man. In the space of just a few days, life had taken on a new meaning and presented him with a sense of purpose he never had before, even through all the years as he climbed through the military ranks to be named a centurion. The only difference was that now he had an eternal perspective…and his first course of action was to talk to Artie.

Notes

1. Deuteronomy 7:6
2. John 3:3
3. Acts 2:1–4
4. Acts 10:45
5. 2 Peter 3:9
6. Romans 10:9
7. Acts 10:48

CHAPTER
14
THE BARRACKS

"Therefore my anxious thoughts make me answer, because of the turmoil within me."

Job 20:2

Barracks living has good points and bad. Camaraderie among the men helps bond them into a cohesive force, but close-quarter living often sacrifices privacy. For the Italian Regiment garrisoned in Caesarea, life was fairly comfortable. As citadels go, this one was above average. Young soldiers such as Artie routinely were housed in the barracks of the citadel, as it generally was where the weapons of war were stored. It was the most fortified building in any city.

As a special attaché to the centurion, Artie was assigned a room with three other men of similar position. The room was rather narrow, certainly longer than it was wide. At one end, the men kept their sleeping mats and personal gear, while at the other, near three small windows stood two long, rough-hewn wooden tables with benches to match. Here the men could clean their weapons, make small talk, mend their garments, and entertain themselves while off-duty with conversation and games of chance. Numerous implements of war and personal protection were neatly placed throughout the room. But its spartan appearance left no doubt this was a man's domain.

Returning to the room after his breakfast the morning after Peter spoke, Artie stood near one of the windows staring out into the distant landscape. These small windows provided little light but played a more significant role as a point of lookout for any approaching enemy during times of siege. His roommates attempted to engage him in a quick game of dice before heading out to their day's assignments, but Artie declined. One remarked that "Artie appears to have lost his best friend," while another generated laughter by making a lewd remark about his love life. Artie simply ignored all such comments and kept his thoughts to himself. They were of yesterday's strange meeting at the home of Cornelius.

"How could an uneducated Hebrew fisherman like Peter change people's minds so quickly?" Artie thought. Peter had appeared to be so logical and precise in his beliefs and so eloquent in relating his facts that even Cornelius seemed ready to accept what he said without further consideration. The resulting change Artie saw in Cornelius and the others appeared to give them an immediate sense of purpose and true happiness. This morning, Artie wondered if he had really heard and seen what was playing over in his mind. He had to admit great puzzlement about the entire episode and wondered why he even seemed a little jealous of what had happened with so many who were there. Most difficult to comprehend was the fact that his centurion, a highly decorated senior officer of Rome, could be swayed by Peter's message. Did not Cornelius find his satisfaction in life from being so successful in his career? With all his military exploits and honors, what more did he need to find fulfillment in life? Even more disturbing to Artie was this question: *How does Cornelius's decision to receive Yeshua relate to my life and career? Will it affect my own dreams of happiness and fulfillment in service to Rome? Could a stigma fall on me because of my close association with him?*

Lost in thought, Artie was unaware when the room suddenly fell silent. Idle chatter among the other soldiers disappeared, replaced by the rapid shuffling of feet as men quickly came to attention. Their commanding officer had entered the room unannounced.

Cornelius scanned the dimly lit room methodically. It had been a long time since, when as a young soldier, he had lived like these men, sharing close quarters in service to Rome. There was a saying that "If you've lived in one barracks, you've lived in them all." "Very true" he mused. The quarters were dark, cramped, and, like all the barracks he had seen in his day, smelled of leather and men.

For a moment he considered the privilege of rank. As a centurion he enjoyed private quarters with attendants, quality furnishings, the best in food rations, and yes, even tasteful aesthetics to soften the harshness of military furnishings. During peacetime you could have your family living with you, which made the life as a Roman officer a bit more pleasant. Though some of his fellow centurions believed such amenities softened a man and weakened his ability to command, Cornelius felt otherwise, and he certainly enjoyed these little trappings of rank and seniority.

With so little light coming from the smoky oil lamps flickering on the table and through the small windows, Cornelius had a difficult time singling-out Artie. Other than saying, "At ease," he spoke nothing to the men. All stood nervously at attention, unsure as to why the highest-ranking officer at the Citadel suddenly had appeared in their midst.

As the silence grew more ominous, Artie slowly came out of his mental fog and turned from his position at the window just as Cornelius's gaze fell upon him. A startled look crossed his face as he snapped to attention, greatly embarrassed by being caught off guard by the presence of the boss. Cornelius spoke: "Articus, a word with you in private!" To the rest he said: "You are dismissed. Report to your workstations!" With smart salutes the other three left, wondering what was going to happen to Artie. After they left the barracks and the two men were alone, Cornelius began to speak: "Walk with me. I want to speak with you as neither your centurion nor your superior, but as one friend talking to another."

CHAPTER
15
THE CONVERSATION

"Listen, for I will speak noble things; And the opening of my lips will reveal right things."
Proverbs 8:6

To avoid the mass of humanity gathered around the main entrance to the Citadel, Cornelius led the way through the little used Tiberius Gate. It was named after Emperor Tiberius himself, who on rare visits to Caesarea liked to use this very gate when he came to inspect the regimental headquarters. He hated the crowds of unwashed humanity who thronged at the public gate, especially the beggars who often lined the walls. These dregs of humanity encased in their dirty rags, voiced plaintive cries for alms while trapped in the stench of their own foul bodies. The Emperor was known to have little use for these unfortunate outcasts of society.

Following the course of the Citadel's outer wall, the two men made their way down the slope of the hill where the fortress stood. They walked on a rocky path of weatherworn stones until finally emerging near a small outcropping of sycamore trees, whose wide-spreading branches afforded much needed shade from the hot morning sun.

Sycamore trees (*Ficus sycomorus*) often were planted along the wayside.[1] Their leaves are heart-shaped, somewhat downy on the underside, and most fragrant. The fruit of this delightful tree is a sweet delicacy to those who partake. Growing in clusters much like grapes and close to the trunk of the tree on little sprigs, they often are plucked and eaten on the spot as a refreshing snack. From high in the trees came the songs of birds, including the tantalizing singsong of the one which seemed to follow Artie everywhere he went. "What is that bird," he thought? "It's almost as though it's trying to say something to me."

Several stone benches were settled among the trees, inviting visitors to sit and converse in relative privacy. After Cornelius extended an invitation for Artie to be seated, the younger soldier awkwardly complied, as always, feeling uncomfortable taking such liberties before his superior.

Cornelius paced back and forth with his hands behind his back, giving the appearance of arranging thoughts in his mind in preparation for a serious discourse. At times he seemed to struggle within himself concerning those thoughts, even on several occasions appearing to be on the verge of making some profound statement to Artie, but quickly returning to his pacing and meditation without speaking.

Artie studied his superior closely, trying to detect any sign that might explain his unusual behavior. During the time he had been in Caesarea, Artie occasionally had felt the centurion wanted to talk to him about something but restrained himself for some unknown reason. Perhaps that was about to happen. At length, Cornelius sat down on the bench across from Artie, cleared his throat, drew a deep breath and began to speak.

"Articus, I want to tell you about a special friend I once had in my life. He too was a centurion and, I might add, a most capable leader of men. Not only was he a friend and fellow officer, but also he once saved me from death's grasp.

"We both were posted here in Caesarea due to an uprising among the Jews who, as you know, greatly resent Roman occupation. Several insurrectionists had infiltrated the city, defying civil authority and the lawful rule of Rome. It seemed that everywhere you turned there was some new group of zealots and thugs attempting to disrupt law and order. Most were self-serving and nothing more than common criminals seeking to line their own purses through thievery while pretending to fight for their people. Added to this general unrest was the paranoia of his Excellency, Pilate, the Governor, toward the various religious and political leaders whom he felt were all after his job.

"Personally, I never cared for Pilate. To me he was part of the problem with the Jews, certainly not part of the solution. He was the fifth procurator of Judea appointed by Tiberius, and one of the worst in my judgment. On more than one occasion his arbitrary administration of justice nearly drove the Jews to revolt. One such time stands out clearly in my mind.

"One of the first acts Pilate did on assuming the Office of Governor was to move Regimental Headquarters from Caesarea to Jerusalem. Of course, the unit took with it their Standard,[2] bearing the likeness of the Emperor. As you may be aware, the religious Jews consider Jerusalem as their 'Holy City,' and the Emperor's likeness violates their law forbidding graven images.[3] No previous official ever had invoked such a hostile action. The streets of Caesarea swelled with Jews from Jerusalem who were demanding the removal of the Standard from their Holy City.

"Pilate was adamant in his decision and ordered us to round up the troublemakers and put them to death if they refused to cease their protest and return to Jerusalem. Fortunately, cooler heads prevailed, and after some tense moments, the governor relented and ordered the Standard returned to Caesarea. I am not sure why he relented, although some say it was because of his wife. The gossip around the city was that she was about the only one who could make him listen to reason and then only occasionally.

"After that, the Governor became even more paranoid and ordered a detachment down to Jerusalem to rout out key troublemakers, insurrectionists, and unseemly lowlifes who, as he put it, were making his life miserable. Truth is, the governor was his own worst enemy when it comes to politics. Evidently, he had never heard the expression that 'wild honey draws more camel flies than bitter gall.' He just did not know how to handle people."

Cornelius continued: "For the better part of a year, I found myself heading up the taskforce in Jerusalem. We were very successful in putting a number of malcontents in chains to await trial on various charges of insurrection. There was one troublemaker who, as far as I was concerned, was just a common criminal. However, he had a reputation among some of the Jews as a powerful force in their fight for freedom from Rome. Some merchants greatly feared him because of his tactic in extorting money from them as protection from riots and other mayhem.

"What I am about to describe occurred on one of those days when the green of the olive trees seemed even greener than usual, and the blue of the sky crisp and mesmerizing. The air was sweet, and we were feeling that it was just a great day to be alive; much like it is here today."

That vivid description caused Artie to draw a full breath of air through his nostrils, conscious of the sweet aroma of the wild honeysuckle bushes nearby. He looked up through the sycamore branches above, catching a glimpse of a cloudless blue sky, and took note of the cool air against his exposed flesh. He spotted a lone yellow bird with wings fully extended riding the wind, then banking sharply to the left, as he no doubt spied a morsel of food to be gained by a quick descent to the earth below. "Is he following me?" Artie wondered.

As Cornelius continued, Artie's thoughts came quickly back to the story being told. He loved to hear of the exploits of seasoned officers who had served Rome throughout their careers. He sat riveted to his seat, absorbing every word spoken by Cornelius while picturing in his mind the scenes being described.

Notes

1. Luke 19:3
2. A Standard is a flag or ensign emblazoned with the official symbol of a particular organization, often used by military or other government units.
3. Deuteronomy 4:16

CHAPTER
16

THE SPECIAL FRIEND

*"A friend loves at all times,
and a brother is born for adversity."*

Proverbs 17:7

"Based on a reliable tip I received, my trusted companion and I went to a small shop on the edge of Fishmonger's row, located just off the street known as Fisherman's Way. Our suspect was said to be using a certain netmaker's shop as a place to hide out from local authorities who were seeking his arrest on sedition and various robbery charges.

"The suspect was known to be of mixed parentage, having a Jewish mother and a Cretan father. We had been told he was a robust man of medium stature, thick through the neck and arms, sporting thick black hair and a heavy beard. He also was reported to be very handy with a seafarer's knife, often boasting of his ability to filet a man as quickly as he could a fish."

Artie could feel the hair stand up on the back of his neck. He loved the thrill of the hunt for enemies of Rome, whether it was on the battlefield as a soldier or in the cities and villages as an officer of the Imperial Crown. That is why he joined the force. He found himself vicariously living the details of the story he was hearing now.

The centurion continued….

"I was point-man entering the small shop, followed closely by my compatriot. Our plan was to act as though we were interested in making a purchase, asking about various types of casting nets while casing the premises in hopes of finding our suspect.

"The shop was a clutter of netting, weights, sea sponges, and implements of the fisherman's trade. Dark and dank, with the smell of stale fish, smoky oil lamps, and sea salt, I was reminded of my disdain both for the fishing business and travel by sea.

"Our survey of the room revealed an elderly Jew seated at a workbench, absorbed in the general repair of a net piled in heaps upon the table before him. His back was bowed, perhaps from countless years of sitting hunched over his netting table. He had one good eye, but the other was clouded and dull, and it appeared to stare off into a sightless distance. He acknowledged our presence with a slight nod of his head but said nothing. With his gnarled fingers he continued to busy himself expertly despite his limited vision, weaving strands of new cord among the salt-soaked broken ones.

"When asked if he were the owner of the shop he replied in the affirmative. The two of us continued to search every nook and cranny of the establishment while pretending to have an interest in a certain style casting weight. Then I slowly circled the small shop looking for evidence of our suspect. In the shop's dim light, I proceeded cautiously with more than a little casual poking here and there with the blunt end of my crowd control crop, which I am afraid tended to identify me as less than a genuine customer.

"I had begun to suspect we had another bad lead regarding information concerning our fugitive when a casting net[1] suspended from an overhead beam at the far corner of the room caught my eye. As I reached toward it—more to inspect the quality of the netting than to examine it as a potential hiding spot—something, or rather someone, suddenly exploded in my face, knocking me to the floor and violently entangling me in the net. I instantly felt a heavy weight upon me, then the sharp pain of a blade of some kind in my left shoulder, followed quickly by a second and then third thrust. I struggled to defend myself from the blows; however, the netting entangled my upper body like a shroud. Though I could not see who my attacker was, I knew immediately that I was in a life and death struggle."

Artie tensed his whole body. His eyes were wide open, and he swallowed hard as his ears took in every word spoken by Cornelius. He let his eyes fall upon the ugly puckered scars carved into the upper left arm of his centurion. "So that's the history of these wounds!" he realized.

Cornelius continued: "I was helpless to defend myself. Had it not been for the quick action of my fellow officer, most certainly I would have met the end of my life there in the tangled net, just as surely as a fish does when snatched from the waters of the sea. Just as I prepared to receive what I knew would be a fatal blow, the weight on my body was lifted as suddenly as it fell upon me. I heard scuffling about me, combined with the crashing of furniture, curses of men, and finally the heavy unmistakable thud of a body hitting the floor next to me. My attacker had been knocked unconscious by repeated blows administered by my companion.

"Quickly turning to my side, my fellow officer helped extricate me from what might have been my shroud and proceeded to examine my wounds. I had serious bleeding from two of the wounds, while the third was less serious. Quickly tearing a piece of cloth from his tunic and pressing it to my wounds, my friend assured me I would live to fight another day. He also said I shouldn't give up soldiering to fish for a living. Despite my anxiety, I had to laugh at his wit.

"Regaining my feet, I was able for the first time to see my attacker's face. To the surprise of neither of us, he was our suspect. On top of me he had seemed like an army of men trying to take my life. But sprawled there on the shop's floor, he didn't look all that foreboding. Unconscious, dirty, and unkempt with blood oozing through his matted black hair, the man looked no different than any other ruffian found on the streets of every large city.

"We quickly bound our prisoner and summoned a detachment of officers to escort him to the garrison. Amazingly, during the whole sordid business the old man at the mending table neither missed a stitch nor showed the slightest emotion at what had just taken place. I guess with him it was just 'business as usual.'

"Artie, I owe my life to my fellow officer. Right now, you may be asking yourself, 'What does this story have to do with why I asked you to accept the mission of escorting the apostle Peter to me from Joppa?' Bear with me. My fellow centurion did not just save my physical life but in many ways, he is responsible for my actions regarding the events of the last few days." Cornelius paused, rose from his seat, closed his eyes then gently rubbed both eyelids with the tips of his fingers.

As he was taking a deep breath and collecting his thoughts, Artie used the quiet moment to ask a question: "What became of your prisoner, sir?"

Turning to Artie and looking him full in the face, Cornelius answered: "I'm glad you asked, for that's an important part of my story. When he was brought before the governor, his Excellency had the man severely flogged and cast into prison, where he remained for more than a year awaiting the death sentence. But then, during the religious observance of what the Jews call *Passover*, he brought the prisoner's name forth to be released from his sentence as a gesture of good will.[2] Though at first it seemed crazy at the time, now it's beginning to make sense to me. The Jewish leaders had brought another man before Pilate whom they accused of wanting to overthrow the government. After multiple trials of that man, Pilate found him innocent of any crime and washed his hands of the matter. Thinking that the Jews would agree with that man's innocence, he presented both the innocent man and the murderous thug for them to choose between. But instead of choosing good over evil, they chose the man who tried to kill me. Incited by their leaders, with one voice they cried out '*BARABBAS!*' *Pilate then said to them, 'What shall I do with Yeshua who is called Christ?' They all said, 'Crucify Him!' Then he asked, 'Why, what evil has He done?' But they kept shouting all the more, saying, 'Crucify Him!'*[3] While not the first time I saw up close the terrifying horror of mob rule, it is a memory I will carry with me to my grave.

"At the time I was so angry at Pilate that for many days my friend kept me away from those who might have reported my anger to the Governor. He was concerned there could be severe consequences to my career or even my life if that had happened. But both he and I knew Rome had put to death a man who had broken no laws and released a common criminal back out on the streets. I am afraid this set a precedent which may haunt law-abiding citizens for centuries to come. Later I heard a rumor that Barabbas had become a follower of *Yeshua*,[4] but I suspect he more likely ended up either receiving due justice from Rome or being run through with a dagger during one of his crimes.

"As for me, I sufficiently recovered from my wounds to resume my duties here in Caesarea. However, had it not been for the expertise of a Greek physician, a Doctor Luke who was in Jerusalem at the time, I probably would not have survived my wounds, and the rescue from my attacker would have been in vain.

"For some mysterious reason, though not themselves life threatening, some wounds never seem to heal, and the skin takes on a reddish-yellow festering, followed by a greenish hue. Red streaks radiate out from the wound and the victim becomes bedfast with feverish hallucinations followed by a torturous death. This was beginning to happen to me.

"Dr. Luke came to the Citadel after my return, for he was known to have a measure of success with problems like that. However, he warned me that perhaps I would find the cure worse than the wounds themselves – and he was right! He ordered that the wounds be washed daily with fresh cloths dipped in seawater, whose properties seem to have therapeutic value. Raw honey then was applied before covering them with clean fresh cloths. The pain I experienced by the sting of salt water on my open wounds was agonizing and seemed to have the effect of opening them afresh each day. It was not so intense that by the fourth or fifth day after the incident, I had become numb to it. I was quite sore for many months and had to be assigned light duty for a time. Eventually I was as good as new. My one regret is that I never got to properly thank the good doctor for his services, and I'm not even sure what became of him. As good as he is I suspect he became the personal physician to some rich or famous personage.

"My fellow centurion, rescuer and friend, later was transferred to Capernaum. It was a good promotion for him but also several days journey from Caesarea. After that we did not get to see each other very often, which was a great disappointment to me. On top of everything his friendship meant to me, he now had saved my life twice!

Notes

1. Casting nets are round or oval with weights around their rim which allow them to sink, thereby catching fish when raised to the water's surface.
2. In part, this offers historical reference for the practice of legal pardons, where a convicted criminal is released without further punishment,
3. Matthew 27:22-23
4. Though this was inferred in a 1961 fictional movie, *Barabbas*, there is no biblical or historical account of his conversion.

CHAPTER
17

LOSS OF A FRIEND

"There is a friend who sticks closer than a brother."
Proverbs 18:24

"Is your friend still in Capernaum?" asked Artie.

"No, he's dead, killed in a common street brawl there. He was trying to restore order among some quarreling factions when he was struck by a stone. He was carried to his bed, where it soon became evident he would not survive. I was notified by special courier and left quickly for Capernaum to be at the bedside of my dying friend."

At this point Artie remembered hearing something Marcus had said back on the beach at Joppa. There, the servant told him his former centurion had died after being hit in the neck and shoulder by a heavy stone which either fell or was thrown from a roof. That prompted him to ask Cornelius, "Was your friend the centurion who was master to Marcus before he became your servant?"

"Yes, that's right," replied Cornelius, "but how did you know?"

"Marcus told me about it the night we spent at the tanner's home in Joppa while we were there getting Peter." Artie went on to tell Cornelius about their encounter, about how neither he nor Marcus could sleep, and provided additional details of their conversation.

"Did he tell you of the life change that came over my friend after his encounter with *Yeshua*?"

"Yes," said Artie, "but I found it hard to believe, and I think Marcus felt the same way also."

Cornelius studied the young man's face, recognizing the strength of Artie's doubt about his friend's life change as well as his disbelief that Marcus could have been healed miraculously at the hand of *Yeshua*.

"Articus, I felt the same way as you when I sat at my friend's bedside, especially when he said his dying would not be the end. He said that when he drew his last breath he immediately would be in heaven with *Yahweh*.[1]

"At that time, I took his words to be those of a man struck on the head and not fully responsible for his thoughts. Although he appeared lucid enough, I have heard many men say some rather strange things on their deathbed.

"My friend implored me to fulfill two deathbed wishes on his behalf. The first concerned Marcus, who is a very humble man and dedicated to serving. My friend implored me to take Marcus as my own and provide a good home for him. He told me about Marcus' near-death illness and the miracle of his healing. It was obvious to me how much he loved his servant and very much wanted him to be well cared-for. To this I readily agreed, and I have found the man to be everything my friend told me.

"His second request related to his concern for my spiritual journey and for a task relating to his own family. Though you didn't know it, your role in bringing Peter to my home finally put the last two pieces of the puzzle together."

That startling statement caused Artie to ask himself, *How could Peter's coming to Caesarea possibly have any connection to a dying man's request concerning Marcus or to me personally?*

Cornelius resumed his pacing back and forth, collecting his thoughts in the process. Artie could see the strain on the centurion's brow and feel the passion in his words as Cornelius reflected on his dead friend's wishes. As for Artie, he never had a friend such as Cornelius described, and, for the most part, did not form close relationships with anyone, male or female. With his father absent most of the time and because his mother died when he was but an infant, he mostly had known only the company of a few relatives who for the most part were simply caregivers. They were kind enough, but never seemed to take a personal interest in him. In turn, he never had been able to relate with anyone from the depths of his heart. Even toward eligible young women he met, he kept at a distance emotionally, moving on once they tried to get serious with him. Artie envied how Cornelius was able to show love and compassion toward his fellow man.

Cornelius returned to his seat, and leaning forward, began to speak:

"My friend had a son he had not seen for many years, one who was but a small infant when he left Rome for duties in faraway places. That boy was the only child of my friend and his young bride, who died in childbirth.

"Torn by the loss of the wife he had loved dearly and having to choose between his duty to the Emperor or caring for his motherless child, he felt the best choice was to leave his son in the care of relatives and friends. Unfortunately, a fighting man must leave his family and endure the pains of uncertainty on the battlefront, which often makes him unable to care for them. Such was the challenge facing my friend. With an urgency to make a choice, he entrusted his infant son to others and departed Rome with his unit.

"Years passed. By the time the battles were over and the occupation of this region was secure, my friend had been absent from Rome for so long he lost track of his son. He was promoted to the rank of centurion, married again, and had several more children. Though he was grateful for a second opportunity to have the family he had so longed for, he never got over the pain of losing his first wife and not knowing the whereabouts of his first-born son. It was a heavy burden for him to bear." Cornelius hesitated, stared straight into the face of Artie, and softly spoke nine words which would forever change the life of Articus.

Notes

1. 2 Corinthians 5:6–8

CHAPTER
18

THE REVEAL

"A father of the fatherless and a judge for widows, is God in His holy habitation."

Psalm 68:5

"My friend was Articus Maximum. He was your father."

Artie did not move a muscle, speak a word, or even breathe for what seemed like an eternity. The blood drained from his face, leaving him "pale as a ghost." He stared at the man who in one short sentence had just caused a rush of emotion to every pore of his body. Numbness spread from his head to his feet in seconds, and suddenly he felt dizzy. He knew he had to force himself to breathe but found it difficult to catch a full breath. Did he hear what he thought he heard? Did Cornelius just tell him that he knew his father, and that his father had been his best friend?

"D-d-d-did you say that your friend was my father?"

"Yes, Artie. On his deathbed he told me how often he had longed to find you and have you at his side. But out of the busyness of life, his guilt for having waited so long to begin the search, and not knowing how or where to begin, he failed to take the steps needed to seek you out and be a father to you.

But after his encounter with *Yeshua* he knew he must find you. 'Whatever it took,' he said. He wanted to find you and ask your forgiveness for not being there for you all those years. He also longed to tell you about the wonderful thing that had happened in his life through coming personally to know *Yahweh*, the God of all creation.

"Articus, your father told me that every day of his life after your birth he thought about you and wished things were different. He wanted to find you and make it up to you somehow, but he never got the chance. It was only a few months after his life-changing experience with *Yeshua* when he was struck down. Just before that occurred, he had secured permission to return to Rome on personal business to search for you. Let me assure you his greatest regret in life was not being there for you as a father.

"Your father made me promise with his last breath that I would find you, tell you of his sorrow, and share the promises of *Yeshua* with you. With his last ounce of strength, he grasped my hand and looked into my eyes, begging me to promise this to him.

"Articus, How could I turn down the wish of a dying man, my good friend? I had no qualms making every attempt to find you, tell you of your father's death and of his great love for you, but I did not understand his religious fervor. Actually, I was not convinced that what he was saying was really true, so I found myself in a quandary.

"After your father died, I made the decision to use what influence I had to seek you out. Because of my position, making discrete inquiries concerning you was no problem. I have many influential friends in Rome, and I sent them private dispatches asking that they quietly obtain your personal information. After what seemed like an eternity, I had what I needed. I learned you had grown into a stalwart young man as interested in serving the Emperor as an officer as was your father. My sources told me you had completed your training with honors and already made quite a name for yourself as a marksman with the javelin and a master of the sword. With those achievements and your physical appearance, it would appear you had a promising career ahead of you. Articus, your father would have been very proud of you.

"Because of your potential, several other units sought your being assigned to them, but I managed to get your orders changed and have you assigned to my regiment as my personal aide. It was no easy matter, and quite a few eyebrows were raised because of your youth and inexperience. But to the best of my knowledge, no one suspected I was fulfilling a deathbed request of your father.

"The second part of my promise to him, telling you about *Yeshua*, was not so easy. I had my own doubts about who the carpenter really was, and I didn't want to tell you about a god I did not believe in myself. That was a real struggle for me.

"For many years I have considered myself a religious man. Articus, any man who has stared death in the face as I have is a fool not to seek a higher purpose to life than just death itself. I found myself praying, wanting to know if the god of the Jews was real. If so, I really wanted to know him and to know what he required of me. Perhaps as a way of 'buying an answer' I tried to show kindness to the Jews and utmost respect for their religion, even giving financial support to their synagogues. I believe you know the rest of the story. I truly believe the visit I received from the angel was *Yahweh*'s answer to my prayers. Peter brought everything into perspective for me. He clearly showed me that what your father experienced in his encounter with *Yeshua* is for all mankind, a personal and intimate relationship with the God of all creation.

"Articus, even while suffering pain and knowing death was imminent, what your father found in *Yeshua* brought him profound happiness and peace of mind. I never have seen a man face death with such a calmness of spirit. Since my encounter yesterday with Peter, I have begun to sense the same peace and joy your father experienced. With a clear conscience I feel I finally can honor your father's request to share his desire for you to experience the same relationship with *Yahweh* that he did.

"It has been a difficult concept for me to understand how *Yahweh* and *Yeshua* can be father and son yet be only one God. I also don't understand how *Yeshua* could be both man and God. Though I don't yet understand these truths, from my own experiences in life I do understand that all men have sinned and fallen short of God's glorious standard.[1] And I believed Peter when he said that only *Yeshua* can bridge the gap between sinful man and the righteousness of *Yahweh*.

"Now I know I could be put to death for what I am about to say, but I still must tell you: I do not believe for a moment that our emperor is a god, even though we are taught to accept this from our youth. I have been in the company of Caesar and have worked at Imperial Headquarters. Believe me when I say that Caesar is just like any other man. He fears death just like you or me and suffers the same doubts in life as we do. Your father told me that *Yeshua* took away those fears and doubts. But it took Peter's message yesterday to reveal to me just who *Yeshua* really is and why He came to earth.

"Articus, in my conversation with Peter and his companions after the meeting ended, they said that *Yahweh* created man to have a relationship with Him, but man broke that relationship when he sinned. It was broken because our Holy God cannot tolerate sin in His presence.² Yet in His love and in His mercy, *Yahweh* sent *Yeshua* to live a sinless life and then to pay the sacrifice for man's sin by His death on the cross. *Yahweh* lived among us so we could see what a perfect life is really like. Yet, *Yahweh* also asked His Son, *Yeshua*, to take upon himself every sin that humans ever have committed, from the time of the first man until the death of the last man who ever will live on earth. Think of that! It was such a horrifying event that while *Yeshua* was on the cross, *Yahweh* withdrew His spirit from *Yeshua*, who cried out, '*Eli, Eli, lama sabachthani?*' *that is,* '*My God, My God, why have You forsaken Me?*'³ If it was so horrifying to *Yeshua* to lose His connection to *Yahweh*; what must that mean to the rest of us to live a life without that relationship?

"As Peter explained it, *Yeshua* took the punishment for our sins so we never would have to go through what He did. His death paved the way for us to have a relationship with *Yahweh* during our earthly lifetime and then to be in heaven with *Yahweh* and *Yeshua* throughout eternity. God Himself paid the price for all our sin. With the price paid, there is nothing left for you or me to do except to accept that payment. We need only to confess with our mouths that *Yeshua* is Lord, and believe in our hearts that *Yahweh* raised Him from the dead. Though it sounds simple, Peter made it clear to me that's all it takes.[4] And he said our decision is so important that *Yahweh* urgently wants each of us to know and believe, because He is not willing that any should perish and face eternity in hell.[5] Son, you know that everyone will die. But through our relationship with *Yahweh*, when we die we step from death into eternal life.[6] Articus, there is no greater gift than knowing we will live forever in heaven with all who have called on the Name of *Yeshua*."[7]

Cornelius paused to let his words sink in. He studied the young man's face for any sign of understanding. There were so many things he longed to tell Articus. For years, he had sensed there just had to be more to life than to live and then die. There were constant nagging questions like: *Why was I born? What is my purpose in life? When and how will I die?* Overriding all those questions was: *What happens at my death?* Cornelius knew all people ask themselves questions like this, maybe not when they are young like Artie, but, as the seasons of life begin to pass, those questions come with more frequency.

Both men remained silent for some time. The only sounds heard were the slight rustle of leaves in the trees spurred on by a slight desert breeze, and the mournful call of yet another lone seagull circling above.

Finally, Artie said, "I need some time to think," without looking at Cornelius. His eyes remained fixed on his boots as he nervously scraped the sand beneath them into a small pile. His erect military posture of before had left him, and he now sat listless and stooped over, seeming to be in a confused state.

He did need time to think about everything that had happened in the last few days. Most especially, he needed to digest all he had learned about the father he never had known.

"I know I have laid a lot on you today, which must be puzzling and bewildering, so I am giving you some time off to think things over. A change in scenery might help, so I will prepare the proper travel documents for you to go to Jerusalem and meet with a friend of mine, a fellow centurion who serves Rome there. He has first-hand knowledge of *Yeshua* and was present at His trial, sentencing, and death by crucifixion. I hope you will listen to everything this man has to say concerning *Yeshua* and what I have told you.

"When you return, if you think I am a madman or for any reason you no longer want to serve in this detachment, you may request a transfer to any other unit of your choice, and I will help that come to pass. Does that seem fair to you?"

"Fair enough, SIR!"

Slowly standing to his feet and regaining his military bearing, he smartly gave the imperial salute of Rome, striking his left breast with his clenched right fist and forearm. "With your permission Sir, I would like to remain here a few moments by myself to contemplate all I have heard."

Returning the salute, Cornelius nodded his assent.

"You're a fine young man and have the makings of a fine officer. You are dedicated to service and know how to show honor where honor is due. We each are acquainted with the troubles that exist in this world, both in men and in forces that are not of flesh and blood. Articus, I now truly believe that *Yahweh* is raising up men who will serve Him in restraining the evils of this world. I have fought diligently for Caesar and Rome all these many years, even when I personally questioned whether the motives of the empire were right. Let it be known that from this day forth I also will serve a Higher Master. Yes, I will continue to honor Caesar in all things which pertain to Caesar, but I likewise will render honor to *Yahweh* in all things that belong to Him. I consider myself a new man in *Yeshua* and a member of 'The Way,' dressed in the uniform of a Roman centurion. *Yeshua* is my Lord, and with all the breath I have left on this earth I shall seek to serve Him."

Leaving Artie to meditate on what he had said, Cornelius departed for his office to prepare the documents Artie would need for the trip to Jerusalem. Closing his office door, he dropped to his knees to pray that *Yahweh* would protect Articus on his journey, giving him wisdom and discernment as he sought the truth about *Yeshua*. After completing the necessary paperwork, he returned to his home to learn more from Peter and the men who had come with him from Joppa.

Notes

1. Romans 3:23
2. Isaiah 59:2
3. Matthew 27:46
4. Romans 10:9
5. 2 Peter 3:9
6. John 5:24
7. Romans 10:13

CHAPTER
19

CORNELIUS & PETER

"You are living stones, being built up as a spiritual house for a holy priesthood, to offer up spiritual sacrifices acceptable to God through Jesus Christ."

1 Peter 2:5

Stepping into his outer courtyard, Cornelius could hear several animated voices from within, coupled with the clatter of plates and smell of food coming from the kitchen. Suddenly he realized it was noontime and that he was hungry. Parting the curtains between the outer and inner courtyards, he saw Peter and his six friends waiting for their meal.

While they waited, Cornelius told Peter about his conversation earlier that day with Articus, and how he broke the news to the young soldier that he had known his father and then told Artie of his own acceptance of *Yeshua*. After listening to that report, Peter agreed with the centurion's decision to send Artie away for a few days to think things through. "Each of those revelations," Peter said, "is sufficient to warrant the need for plenty of quiet time and a change of scenery to process."

Moving on in their conversation, Cornelius told Peter he understood that his acceptance of *Yeshua* as the son of

Yahweh was all that was required for him to be adopted into *Yahweh's* family as His child.[1] But as a new follower of *Yeshua*, he wanted to know more about how one should live.

Peter began by advising him that even though the peace he had received by accepting *Yeshua* as his Savior "surpassed all understanding,"[2] he should be prepared for various trials that would test his faith like fire tests gold.[3] "Furthermore," said Peter, "you as well as all believers must keep 'sober in spirit,' prepare your minds for action, and fix them completely on the grace offered by *Yeshua*. Believers often find this a challenge at first, but you need to work hard at not being lured by the carnal lusts which plague all of mankind. I certainly did find this to be a challenge!"[4]

At this juncture Cornelius called for Marcus, a trained scribe, to join the meeting and take notes. The centurion felt these written notes would be useful for his own reflection and for reaching others with the good news of salvation. Once Marcus was seated with pen and papyrus,[5] Peter again began to speak.

He said that the starting point of being a follower of *Yeshua* is to have a sincere love for all other believers, regardless of their station in life. Referring to his former comment about "being lured by carnal lusts," Peter said that to love others we must "put aside all malice, deceit, hypocrisy, envy and slander." He commended Cornelius for wanting to spend time with him and the other believers who had accompanied him from Joppa and commented that just like newborn babies need nourishment, so do new believers. "But," he said, "that nourishment is not from food, but from seeking out and spending time with those who are knowledgeable and willing to teach what *Yeshua* taught."[6]

Then Peter began a new line of thought which seemed incomprehensible to Cornelius. He said that *Yeshua* is like the cornerstone of a giant building, such as a temple, and believers are being built by *Yahweh* into "living stones" of a spiritual temple. Then Peter went further by saying that believers actually are *Yahweh's* "holy priests" ... in fact, a "kingdom of priests." Because of this, Cornelius and the others who had become believers needed to give special attention to how they live among non-believers. Peter said that if non-believers saw honorable behavior in the believers they might believe and give honor to *Yahweh*. [7]

This admonition was to Cornelius like a lightning stroke out of a clear sky! As a centurion and Rome's official representative in Caesarea, he dealt daily with soldiers under his command, other Roman officials, Jewish leaders, and citizens-at-large. He often had to enforce the law, even enacting harsh punishment when prescribed. Would being a believer stand in the way of administering his oath of allegiance to Rome?

As if he knew what Cornelius was thinking, Peter said: "*Yeshua* teaches that for His sake, we are to accept all authority—the king as head of state, and the officials he has appointed. Furthermore, we are to show respect for the king and accept the authority of all who are over us, even if they are harsh and unreasonable. That may cause us to suffer at times, but we must remember that *Yeshua* also suffered, even though He did not sin. The good news is that He left

His case in the hands of *Yahweh*, who always judges fairly... and we must also!"[8]

The next subject Peter addressed was how friends of new believers would react to their changed patterns of behavior. As a man whose entire adult life had been spent in the raucous and often bawdy military environment, Cornelius wondered how he would continue to fit into that world, and what difficulties it would pose if he witnessed to others in the military, including young soldiers like Articus.

Peter said most would not understand his new way of living, though those under his command would say nothing to his face. The greatest challenge in the military would be for those of lesser rank who would be teased, called names, and harassed for not doing the immoral and lustful things they had done before becoming believers. Another challenge might come from higher commanders putting a gag order on the spread of religious beliefs. "Even so," said Peter, "It is no shame to suffer for being a follower in The Way. The time is coming when those who put you and others down for believing in *Yeshua* will have to face *Yahweh*, who will judge everyone, both the living and the dead.[9] And what terrible fate awaits those who never have believed in *Yeshua*." Peter concluded his remarks with this encouragement: "Give all your worries and cares to *Yahweh*, for He cares about what happens to you!"[10]

About that time, servants bearing dishes with savory fragrances began invading the room, signaling it was time to eat. Marcus breathed a sigh of relief, for he was tired of having to listen so closely to write everything down. *Why did I ever learn to write?* he mused. *There were other things I'd planned to do with my time this afternoon! At least I've been invited to eat with this group instead of serving them, so I guess there's some compensation for my writing skills!*

Perhaps sensing Marcus' negative attitude, Peter said this before they ate: "Be careful! Watch out for attacks from the devil, your great enemy. He prowls around like a roaring lion, looking for some victim to devour!" That statement caused Marcus to shudder. He thought: *Lions don't roar until they find their prey.*[11] *So if the devil prowls around like a roaring lion, that means he's already found his victim! Could that be true? Am I in the devil's sights?* Marcus quickly put that thought out of his mind as he wanted to enjoy his meal without getting heartburn!

It had been a long day for Cornelius, beginning with the difficult conversation he had with Articus and followed by intense teaching from Peter. After the meal he adjourned the group for the evening, saying they would reconvene the next day after he completed pressing duties at the Citadel.

Notes

1. Romans 8:15
2. Philippians 4:7
3. 1 Peter 1:6–7
4. 1 Peter 1:13–14
5. Papyrus originated in Egypt several centuries before Christ and is made from the pithy stem of a water plant found in the Mediterranean region.
6. 1 Peter 2:1–2
7. 1 Peter 2:4–12

8. 1 Peter 2:13–23
9. 1 Peter 4:5
10. 1 Peter 4:1—5:7
11. Psalms 104:21

CHAPTER
20

THE DAY OF THE LORD

"We did not follow cleverly devised tales when we made known to you the power and coming of our Lord Yeshua Christ, but we were eyewitnesses of His majesty."

2 Peter 1:16

Peter's teaching the next day was just as intense as it had been the day before.

Once more he began with an encouraging thought, "As we get to know *Yeshua* better, His divine power gives us everything we need for living a godly life. In fact, we will receive His own glory and goodness. Not only that, you will learn as you grow in His teachings that He has given us many rich and wonderful promises. One of His best promises is giving the *Holy Spirit* to help us escape the decadence all around us caused by evil desires and lust for worldly things, and His grace to forgive us when we give in to those desires." Cornelius thought of all the things he had done in his climb to becoming a centurion. Many were honorable, but to his shame, some were not, especially those driven by greed and envy. If Peter's words were to be taken at face value, Cornelius and other believers should quit trying to steer their own course, choosing instead to let *Yahweh* be their commander through the *Holy Spirit*. Somehow, that was very comforting to the centurion.

Throughout the day, Peter taught many things useful to becoming more and more like *Yeshua*, but two major teachings had the most impact on Cornelius. First was a system which, Peter said, if used would prevent believers from ever stumbling or falling away in their faith. That system is this:

"Since we have received all Yahweh's precious promises, we must apply all diligence to our faith, practice moral excellence, apply knowledge to that excellence, exercise self-control, strive for perseverance and godliness, add brotherly kindness to our godliness, and in that practice love. If these qualities are ours and are increasing, they render us useful and fruitful in the true knowledge of our *Yeshua*. Those who lack these qualities either are blind or short-sighted, having forgotten his purification from his former sins. Therefore, be all the more diligent to make certain about His calling and choosing you; for as long as you practice these things, you will never stumble; for in this way the entrance into the eternal kingdom of our Lord and Savior *Yeshua* Christ will be abundantly supplied to you.[1] Faith, moral excellence, knowledge, self-control, perseverance, godliness, brotherly kindness and love."

As a military commander, Cornelius liked and was accustomed to well-thought-out procedures and protocols. *Yahweh's* system of actions, built one-on-the-other, appealed to his sense of orderliness. "I can follow that system, and it is something I can teach others" he thought to himself. "More than anything else I can see that *Yahweh* is a God of order, not chaos.² That is right in line with what I've been taught and are the policies of Rome. This is good!"

Over lunch, Peter told of a remarkable experience he had with *Yeshua* and two other apostles, the brothers James and John. He said *Yeshua* had taken the three of them up on a high mountain³ where they witnessed a most remarkable sight: Moses and Elijah (deceased Hebrew leaders and prophets from centuries ago) appeared in visible form, and *Yeshua* was changed from human form into a heavenly body and then back to human form.⁴ Peter said that experience enabled him and all believers to gain better understanding of our ability to recognize family and friends in heaven. Since Moses and Elijah knew what was happening on earth, perhaps we too will have that kind of knowledge. Most important, *Yeshua* demonstrated what many believers have wondered, *Is it possible for our bodies to return to human form at the resurrection after they have decayed and turned to dust? Yeshua's* transfiguration demonstrated that truth. Cornelius couldn't help but marvel that he was in the presence of one of only three living humans who had witnessed one of the most remarkable events of all time! With this understanding, Cornelius knew that whatever happened to his body after death, it would be made whole again when *Yeshua* returned at His second coming.

As the sessions with Peter drew to a close, the apostle reminded all present that there would be scoffers who didn't believe in the deity of *Yahweh* or of *Yeshua*, asking "Where is he?" He then told them to remember that "…*a day is like a thousand years to Yahweh, and a thousand years is like a day.*"⁵

He also told them about events which would take place at the end of time as man knows it, and encouraged them that regardless of what might happen, simply to live pure and blameless lives and be at peace with *Yahweh*. His closing thought was this: *"Be on your guard so that you are not carried away by the error of unprincipled men and fall from your own steadfastness, but grow in the grace and knowledge of our Lord and Savior, Yeshua."*[6]

With lunch over, Cornelius returned to his office to make certain all the papers Articus would need for his trip to Jerusalem were in order. Later, after the evening meal, because he had early meetings at the Citadel the next morning, he said his "Goodbyes" to Peter and his six friends and retired to his private quarters. There he joined his wife, Cassia, for raisin cakes and a goblet of wine while they relaxed and talked over Peter's visit and what it meant to them and their household.

"Cassia, to think *Yahweh* would have noticed my prayers and charitable gifts to the Jews and send an angel specifically to me, a non-Jew, is beyond my comprehension! What is even more amazing is that he told me exactly who I needed to contact, where Peter could be found, and that Peter would come at just my bidding; that is something I never would have dreamt in my fondest expectations!"

Cornelius further reflected on what Peter's coming, his message, and the giving of the *Holy Spirit* meant to them and to all present who had heard and believed. Cornelius loved his two sons, Cyrus and Titus and their families, and rejoiced that all now were together as believers and would be throughout eternity. He went on: "Cassia, you know how long I have been searching for the truth as to whether or not there was one true God. Though my support of Jewish needs and my prayers on their behalf were not for selfish or personal reasons, nonetheless *Yahweh* took note of them and gave us this incredible blessing. All my life I have sought truth and justice, and I believe this special gift has been given to me...to us...to use insofar as possible in my position to make others know that He loves us non-Jews as much as the Jews. I feel like a sponge—wanting not just to soak up what Peter has brought to our household—but to 'wring it out' to make *Yeshua's* message known to many more."

Finally, exhausted from his long sessions with Peter and what he had learned, Cornelius changed into his sleep tunic ready for bed. As he drifted off to sleep, he silently thanked *Yahweh* for *Yeshua* and Peter, and asked the *Holy Spirit* to continue teaching and guiding him throughout the remaining days of his life.

Notes

1. 2 Peter 1:3–12
2. Isaiah 45:18
3. Thought to be in the vicinity of Caesarea, earlier scholars suggested Mt. Tabor while modern scholars think it was probably Mt. Hermon.
4. Scriptures relating to the transfiguration include Matthew 17:1–8; Mark 9:2–8; Luke 9:28–36; 2 Peter 1:16–18, and John 1:14.
5. 2 Peter 3:8
6. 2 Peter 3

CHAPTER

21

ROMULUS

> *"Are You the Christ, the Son of God?*
> *Yeshua said to him, 'You have said it yourself; Nevertheless I tell you, thereafter you will see the SON OF MAN SITTING AT THE RIGHT HAND OF POWER, and COMING ON THE CLOUDS OF HEAVEN."*
>
> Matthew 26:63–64

Artie's arrival in Jerusalem marked his first visit to the place known to the Jews as the "City of God." Sometimes called "Zion" or simply "Salem" (which means "peace" in Hebrew), Jerusalem was steeped in ancient religious tradition and was a city full of mystery and intrigue. Located on a high ridge some thirty-two miles from the Dead Sea, eighteen from the river Jordan, twenty from Hebron, and thirty-six miles from the city of Samaria, Jerusalem was naturally fortified. The main water supply was derived from a perennial spring, and the city appeared to be almost impregnable from attack due to deep ravines on the east, south and west sides. Artie thought to himself, *Perhaps these are the reasons why the Jewish king, David, favored this as the site where he would build his palace and governmental offices and establish his throne.*

Unlike Rome, Jerusalem seemed to have been put together in haphazard fashion without much preplanning. The narrow streets forced people to walk in single file, and alleys running off the streets were even more narrow. The houses were built right up against each other with little space between them and the streets. There seemed to be no order to the layout of the streets, making it difficult for newcomers to find their way around. The dirt streets were full of rubbish—bricks, broken bits of pottery and refuse of all kinds—and Artie could tell they would become a muddy quagmire when it rained or snowed. He also sensed that garbage and human waste would be so foul in warm weather that wealthier people would go to summer homes outside the city. But Artie's task this day was not to evaluate Jerusalem as a place to live or work. Rather, he was on a mission which might become the most important one of his life.

True to his word, Cornelius had prepared extensive written orders for Artie to travel to Jerusalem, which was several days' journey from Caesarea. They called for him to report to the Citadel to the office of the centurion who had witnessed the death of *Yeshua* of Nazareth. Artie was not sure how he felt about that appointment. He had never met such a high-ranking centurion, and he felt more than a little awkward asking a senior officer about a death he had overseen by crucifixion on a cross of a man who had died like a common criminal. Even more concerning to him was asking the centurion what his thoughts were when he was purported to have said, "Truly that man was the Son of *Yahweh*."[1] Artie was afraid the centurion or others present might think of him as a lunatic or a fanatic. Yet something within him was compelling him to seek out answers, and that gave him the courage to go ahead with his search.

Artie's two-day walk from Caesarea to Jerusalem left him ill-prepared to see the centurion immediately, so, after presenting his credentials to guards at the front gate of the Jerusalem Citadel, he asked where he could bathe and put on a fresh uniform. When those chores were completed, he was directed to the office of the centurion's chief of staff, who notified the centurion of Artie's arrival. After a short wait, he was ushered into the grand and opulent office of Romulus Verelli, Senior Centurion in Jerusalem for the Eastern District. This important post included the security of the Office of His Excellency, Marcus Antonius Felix, Roman procurator of Judea, whose appointment came directly from Emperor Tiberius. Romulus had specific responsibility for the protection and orderly procedures of trial courts in the Roman occupational government. More specifically, he was charged with administering the sentence of crucifixion to state prisoners. This was a job he had dutifully performed…until recently.

Romulus was a powerfully built man. Though not tall, his arms, chest and legs were massive. He reminded Artie of a Greek wrestler whose center of gravity made him an ideal warrior for hand-to-hand combat. He was the kind of man you would want guarding your back in a street fight, definitely as a friend rather than a foe. He looked as if he could easily take on any ten men at one time in a free-for-all. Adding to his intimidating look was his completely bald head and a rather raw and nasty two-inch scar located above his left eye. The wound had not been properly closed, and had healed leaving a wide, deep scar roughly in the shape of a Roman numeral five (V).

"Come in young soldier. Articus Maximus is it? Earlier in my career I knew another centurion with that name; are you related to him?"

"Yes, he was my father, but no longer living."

After expressing proper condolences, Romulus said, "I have been expecting you. I trust your journey from Caesarea was without incident. With all the traffic on the road from Caesarea, one never knows what to expect. It seems like the roads forever are under construction with detours that are both time-consuming and hard on chariots. Instead of working, the slaves just seem to be standing around waiting for someone to tell them what to do. A fine group of lazy louts in my opinion; you'd think they are all foremen from the way they act! Not only that, but the roads are also just getting too busy and crowded. I miss the old days when a man could travel for miles without seeing another soul on the road. Even the food you get at wayside inns seems as if little thought is given to its preparation, as if there is no pride in being a cook. When I was younger, we soldiers used to hunt for small game on our journeys and prepare our own meals. But with an expanding population and so many traveling, wild game is nowhere to be found. I tell you, young man, it's not like the old days. Now, while my staff brings us some refreshments, tell me about your journey and why you have come." With that remark, Romulus clapped his hands to summon a servant who materialized instantly. After receiving instructions for the refreshments, the servant departed as quickly as he had come.

Artie found the senior officer's musing of "the good old days" both frustrating and a little irritating. "Not the level of conversation I would have with a junior officer if I were a centurion," he thought.

Responding to Romulus' question about his trip, Artie first thanked him for making time in his schedule to meet with him, apologizing for the disruption. "Nonsense my young friend," said Romulus, "I am glad to accommodate the wishes of my good friend, Cornelius. I am sure he would offer me the same courtesy if I should require such."

About that time, the servant reappeared with fig cakes and wine. Romulus told him the figs came right from the Kidron Valley outside Jerusalem, but the "fruit of the vine" was imported from "Mother Rome." Touting its virtues, Romulus insisted that "No finer nectar of the grape is elsewhere to be found, with such excellent color and bouquet as well as a delight to the lips and palate." At this point Artie began to realize why Romulus seemed to be so relaxed in the conversation. The centurion had been enjoying a cup of wine when Artie had entered the room, and he already seemed a bit tipsy. Since it was only mid-morning, Artie wondered if Romulus, knowing the conversation would take him back to the fateful day of *Yeshua's* crucifixion, needed the wine to help calm him while discussing those painful memories.

Romulus began by saying, "The dispatch the courier brought from Cornelius asks that I provide you with information I have concerning a certain prisoner named *Yeshua*, who was under my charge before he was crucified in Jerusalem some time back. Is this correct?"

"Yes Sir, it is. My centurion believes *Yeshua* was different than other men who have been put to death on a cross. He also has told me my own father, about whom I know very little, was acquainted with *Yeshua*. If you still recall the man and information leading up to his crucifixion, I would like to know as much as you remember about this carpenter from Nazareth."

"Of course," said Romulus. "Since we'll be talking for a while, let's move out to the portico under the palms. Perhaps we can find a little breeze and a bit of relief from this miserable heat. Oh, how I long for the temperate hills of Rome and the beautiful gardens of my family villa. What sacrifices one must make to be a man of the sword in service to Caesar!" With that remark, Romulus upended his goblet and drained the last drop of wine with a smack of his lips and a gesture of satisfaction. Placing the goblet on a table, with somewhat wobbly steps he led the way to the portico.

Once out in the open-air, Romulus invited Artie to take a seat in a very comfortable chair of polished olive wood. It had been expertly carved to accommodate the form and structure of a man and was padded with cushions of fine cloth woven with intricate designs of pomegranates and grapes. It was, perhaps, the finest chair on which the young soldier ever sat. Romulus rested his own rather large frame in a similar chair located nearby.

As Romulus had hoped, a soft breeze stirred the air, reviving him somewhat while giving animation to the fronds of the palm trees clustered about the seating area. Like what Artie had experienced at Cornelius' home, the trees were planted in large containers so as to be portable and positioned strategically about the patio as needed for shade or entertainment. Several other planters of varying sizes, overflowing with an array of beautiful flowers and greenery, were positioned around the porch.

Several stone benches invited guests to relax near a large ornamental basin replete with fresh water flowing from a small aqueduct that entered the patio from the north wall, spilling out of the basin, and exiting through the south wall. The sound of the splashing water lent a soothing, relaxing touch to the scene. Small brightly colored fish darted toward the water's surface as Romulus tossed a few heads of grain into the basin.

"Do I assume you never have witnessed a crucifixion?" asked Romulus of Artie. "If not, I assure you it is a gruesome and troubling experience, not for either the squeamish or fainthearted. It is an assignment that neither I nor most I know relish in any way. As for me, I would much rather see a man meet his end on the field of battle than as a prisoner of the state. However, duty is duty, and I have always followed my orders to the letter.

"In my many years as a soldier of Rome I have seen many crucifixions, but none can compare with that of the Jewish carpenter. There were many strange things which took place that day for which neither I nor anyone else can offer logical explanations. Many who were there that day heard me plainly state, 'Truly, this man was the Son of *Yahweh*.' Whether my outburst was the result of what I was witnessing or a manifestation of *Yahweh* himself, I cannot say. But I cannot offer any rational thoughts for what I saw and heard that day.

"The events leading up to that strange day began the day before when I was assigned to accompany some Jewish priests and temple guards to a small garden just a short distance out of town. I was told that an informant would lead us to the hiding place of a man who was accused of trying to incite the Jews against their established religion and to usurp the authority of Rome. It also was asserted that the defendant claimed not only to be the son of their god, but also that he would supplant Caesar as supreme ruler. If true, that would have made him guilty of treason and insurrection.

"We located the suspect across the Kidron Brook from Jerusalem in a place known as Gethsemane. It is a small clearing among the olive groves sometimes used for pressing oil from the olives and a favorite location for people hoping to escape the heat and noise of Jerusalem. While I had hoped for an element of surprise, this was not possible because of the large crowd carrying clubs and swords which had been stirred up by the Jewish leaders. As the saying goes, 'They made enough noise to awaken the dead.' I didn't like it, but we were under order not to interfere with Jewish religious leaders and practices. I and the soldiers with me were there just to keep order if fighting broke out. Fortunately, there was none, though things did get out of hand for a moment."

"What happened?" asked Artie, sensing that the story was about to get interesting.

"What happened?!" said Romulus. "I'll tell you what happened! That fool of a servant to the High Priest got too close to one of *Yeshua's* rabble rousers, who cut off the servant's ear with his sword. Before anyone could react to that vicious attack, *Yeshua* said: '*Put your swords away. Do you not know that I can call on my Father and He will at once put at My disposal more than twelve legions of angels? This is not the way it will happen.*'[2] Then *Yeshua* reached up, touched where the ear had been, and completely restored it as though nothing had happened. One minute the man was wounded, bleeding, and screaming in pain, and the next minute it was as though nothing had happened![3] No wound, nothing. Not even a scar. I thought to myself, *Did I just see what I thought I saw, or was it a trick of some kind?"*

By now Artie was concerned that Romulus's continued drinking might prevent his remembering the information Artie wanted so desperately. And he was beginning to wonder if the unprecedented events of that crucifixion day had caused Romulus to turn to drink to forget.

Continuing his account, Romulus said: "Whatever it was, I know that in an instant all the friends of *Yeshua* scattered like mice in every direction, leaving only dust in their paths. I have never seen people run so fast. But since we had our man in custody, we didn't bother to go after the others. Our mission was accomplished, and *Yeshua* gave us no problems.

"There was another strange thing about his arrest: he appeared to know everything that was going to happen, almost as though he had planned it all in advance, and he seemed more in control of the situation than we were. I felt like he was the one in charge of the whole sordid business, rather than either the Temple police or my own men. It was weird, I tell you."[4]

Artie furrowed his brow as he tried to get a sense of what the scene must have been for Romulus. Certainly, what he heard to that point whetted his appetite for more information.

Just then Romulus's servant, accompanied by two others, arrived with more fig-cakes and wine, plus an array of fresh fruit which included slices of succulent melon, ripe berries, and apricots. A platter of salted dry sea bass and several small loaves of a brown hard bread known as *fortusha* completed the service. Artie could not remember ever having been entertained so well. To him it was embarrassing for such a low-ranking officer as he to be treated so royally. Not so for Romulus.

"It's about time you came," Romulus complained to the servants, "my goblet is empty." Both men waited in silence as the servants offered each man his choice of the delicacies. The wine was in bronze goblets on a bronze tray, which was offered first to Romulus, which he quickly accepted. Quaffing it down in one gulp, he proffered the empty goblet to the servant, who once again filled it from an ornate decanter until his master signaled that he'd had enough. The tray then was presented to Artie, who likewise drained his goblet, then held it out for the servant to fill again.

With a polite smile and nod, Artie communicated his thankfulness to the servant before once again turning his attention to his host. Romulus studied the contents of his goblet silently until the servants were gone. Slowly draining the cup, holding the wine against his tongue for some moments before swishing the nectar around his mouth, he then tilted his head back, closed his eyes and swallowed ever so slowly, as if completing a formal ritual. A smile of deep satisfaction crept from the corners of his mouth as he pronounced judgment on this fruit of the vine. "Ah! What beauty, what taste! A good wine can only be compared to the loveliness of a fair maiden." With that he motioned once again for his cup to be filled and waited impatiently for the servant to comply.

While Romulus' attention was focused on the wine, Artie sensed the fluttering of a small bird's wings as it landed on a nearby stone fountain. It was another of the small yellow birds which seemed to be following him. *Is it my imagination*, he asked himself, *or is it an omen of some kind?*

Just then Romulus attention returned to the present and he asked, "Where was I my young friend? Oh yes, the arrest."

"We took our suspect to the Office of the High Priest, a man named Caiaphas. Actually, we first stopped at the home of Annas, his father-in-law and the real power behind the position of High Priest. Once Annas heard the complaint, he sent us on to see his son-in-law, Caiaphas, who held the official position of High Priest. My observation even then was that this fellow *Yeshua* didn't stand a chance. The entire political body of the Jewish State, the *Sanhedrin*, were falling all over themselves trying to find any witnesses who could give clear testimony about this man's guilt. Though that group supposedly is comprised of the Jews' top legal scholars, known as the *Sadducees*, and the strict religious leaders known as *Pharisees*, I have never seen so many shady characters, street bums, and bribed individuals giving such flimsy testimony to a legal body. Though it didn't mean anything to me what they decided, it looked like the whole city of Jerusalem was determined to convict the carpenter regardless of the truth. Finally, the *Sanhedrin* put forth two men claiming that *Yeshua* had threatened to destroy the Temple of *Yahweh* and then rebuild it again in just three days. If true, that testimony alone should have told everyone present that they were dealing with a man who was not rational. My teacher and mentor at the garrison academy used to say, 'People like that need help, not prosecution.' Everyone knows it took years to build that temple. How could someone destroy it and then completely rebuild it in just three days? I ask you now, how?"

Artie just shook his head and took another sip of wine. Though it was excellent, he preferred what could be purchased on his salary, a working man's wine called "Vineyard's Farm."

As he watched Romulus consume far too much wine and witnessed the slurring of his speech, he began to wonder if he ever would hear the full account of *Yeshua's* crucifixion. Perhaps his role as Chief Executioner in the death of *Yeshua* had robbed him of the ability to think clearly and act logically.

Romulus continued: "The High Priest asked *Yeshua* to defend himself on the charges, but he stood silent, seemingly resigned to the accusations. Finally, Caiaphas asked him directly, 'Are you the *Messiah*, the Son of *Yahweh*?' He asked this question with contempt in his voice and a smirk on his face as if to telegraph to the officials and politicians present, 'Let's see what this pretender has to say about himself.' Caiaphas was certain he had trapped *Yeshua* with that question.

"Then *Yeshua* said something I still don't understand. He looked at Caiaphas and the whole crowd and said, '*Yes, it is as you say. I say to all of you, in the future you will see the Son of Man sitting at the right hand of the Mighty One and coming on the clouds of heaven.*'[5] That was the final straw for the High Priest. He tore his clothes, screamed, and yelled 'Blasphemy! Blasphemy! What need do we have of more witnesses?' His response incited the crowd who began to spit on *Yeshua*, slap him and demand his death. A mob developed so quickly that if my men had not stepped in to quell them, they would have killed *Yeshua* right then and there.

"Am I making any sense to you, soldier? I know I get a little excited when I tell what happened; sometimes I even have to ask myself if it did." As if to take a breather before going on, he turned back to the refreshments and offered them to Artie who politely refused, hoping Romulus would resume his account of that fateful day.

Notes

1. Mark 15:39
2. Matthew 26:52–54
3. Luke 22:49–51
4. Mark 14; Luke 22; John 18
5. Matthew 26:64

CHAPTER

2 2

STANDING IN THE DOCK[1]

*Pilate asked Yeshua, saying,
"Are You the King of the Jews?"*

And He answered him and said, "It is as you say." Then Pilate said to the chief priests and the crowds, "I find no guilt in this man."

Luke 23:3–4

Picking up where he left off, Romulus told Artie that he and his men hastened to take *Yeshua* from there before the Jews killed him. "They (the Jews) headed for the Governor's Palace, since Pilate was the principal Roman authority over Jerusalem, saying, 'We need his authorization before anybody can be put to death.'

"The Governor was not very happy to be awakened from his sleep, and quickly made it known. I think the only reason he agreed to a hearing was because of his paranoia that someday he might be replaced as Governor. What really got his attention was when he was told our prisoner was trying to set himself up as a king. Pilate is just like you and me, young soldier, if we think someone is after our jobs, we will do anything to prevent it from happening.

"By an unusual coincidence, King Herod was in Jerusalem at the time. Normally, Pilate would not have looked on that with favor, since relationships between the two men were strained. But when the Governor found out the prisoner was a Galilean, a subject of Herod and alleged to have called himself 'King,' he decided to send *Yeshua* to Herod for him to hear the case. In that way Pilate would eliminate dealing with the Jews on such a contentious matter, and Herod could see with his own eyes and hear with his own ears the 'miracle worker' who had all Judea in such an uproar.

"The Governor did accomplish the latter. Herod had heard of *Yeshua* and hoped he would 'perform some tricks and miracles.' But when *Yeshua* refused to cooperate, he was soon sent back to Pilate. For his part, Herod seemed pleased that Pilate deferred to him, and the two have since become closer. Of course, Herod's refusal to hear the case meant another trip across town for a second audience with Pilate. This time, as *Yeshua* stood officially in the dock, Pilate interrogated him more thoroughly about the charges against Him, asking point blank, 'Are you king of the Jews?' *Yeshua* instantly replied, '*Yes, it is as you say.*'[2]

"Though other charges were made against him by his Jewish accusers, *Yeshua* refused to answer or even acknowledge them. As I said earlier, he just seemed to accept their case against him without any defense at all. It was almost as if he had a death wish or something. I still do not understand it.

"I could tell that Pilate really was concerned about the situation. We heard later that Pilate's wife sent him a message asking him to have nothing to do with *Yeshua*. Seems as though she had a vivid dream where *Yeshua* was called "a righteous man," and she told Pilate to have nothing to do with the case.[3] Even disregarding her dream, I believe he didn't see this unassuming Jewish carpenter as a threat to either the Jewish or Roman political system or to his position as Governor. I think he would have preferred ordering that *Yeshua* be given a good flogging for stirring up the Jews and then dismissing the whole group from his presence. But he found himself in the dilemma of wanting to do what was reasonable while having to treat the Jewish leadership with kid gloves. He had been reprimanded by Rome a time or two for charges of mishandling matters with them, and he didn't need any more problems. After thinking things over for a while, Pilate finally came up with a solution.

"It was Pilate's custom as a goodwill gesture to release a prisoner during the time of feast. Since a notorious prisoner named 'Barabbas' was awaiting execution, Pilate supposed that if given a choice between releasing either a hardened criminal like him or a religious dissident like *Yeshua*, they surely would choose to free *Yeshua*. So, he said to them, '*Whom do you want me to release for you? Barabbas, or Yeshua who is called Christ?*'"[4]

The mention of the name 'Barabbas' got Artie's attention. "Is this the same Barabbas who attacked Cornelius a couple of years back and almost ended his life?" "The very same one," responded Romulus.

"In response to Pilate's question, the whole crowd shouted 'Barabbas! Barabbas! at the top of their lungs. Then Pilate asked them, 'What shall I do with *Yeshua*? What crime has he committed?' Once more with one loud voice the whole crowd shouted again and again, 'Crucify him, crucify him!'

"You could tell this really upset Pilate, for he knew the carpenter did not deserve death. But when he saw they were about to riot and weren't about to change their minds he asked for a basin of water, washed his hands in front of the crowd and said, '*I am innocent of this Man's blood; see to that yourselves.*' And all the people said, '*His blood shall be on us and on our children!*' The die was cast. Pilate called for Barabbas to be released and turned *Yeshua* over to us to be flogged prior to crucifixion.[5]

"Artie, even in your few years of service to Rome, you have come to understand that soldiers don't ask questions, we just obey our orders. That was the situation in which I found myself regarding 'the Carpenter King.' I knew *Yeshua* had done nothing worthy of death—it was a frame-up on the part of enemies who had greater standing with the authorities than he—but I had no choice in the matter. As the chief Roman military officer in Jerusalem, it was my duty to see his sentence through to completion.

"In defense of Pilate and myself, *Yeshua* has to accept part of the blame. In the first place, he should have known that constant criticism of his own religious leaders wouldn't set well with them. His ideas which seemed to be at odds with their established system of religious practices had gotten many of the people all stirred up. And when he appeared before Herod and Pilate, why didn't he speak and offer a defense of some kind? Why did he just stand there like some sort of martyr... and what about the friends who were with him? When things got rough, they just disappeared.

"Though I've never admitted it to anyone else, I truly am ashamed of letting things get out of hand when we got back to headquarters. I never should have allowed the entire cohort[6] to be present and participate in his humiliation. When you bring 500 soldiers together in any unsupervised situation, it's easy for things to get out of hand. After stripping him naked, from somewhere they found a scarlet robe they put on him. Then someone twisted a crown of thorns, put it on his head, and stuck a reed in his right hand. Those nearest him knelt and mocked him, saying, '*Hail, King of the Jews!*' After that they spit on him, took away the reed and beat him on the head, retrieved the scarlet robe and dressed him in his own shabby clothes. Then I chose an elite *conturbenium*[7] especially trained to handle executions like this and prepared for the journey to Golgotha."[8]

Articus felt a sense of revulsion learning that a man condemned to die had been tortured and humiliated by a cohort of Roman soldiers. He hated to think that fellow officers like himself could become a pack of sadistic bullies when given the opportunity. Yes, he too enjoyed having a good time, often making fun of his army buddies. However, he found it loathsome that any man could enjoy torturing and even adding to the suffering of others. "Killing your enemy in combat, killing as a means to protect the empire or enforcing the laws of the land is one thing, but enjoying it as sport is quite another." His own blood ran cold at the thought!

Suddenly he realized that his negative thoughts were reflected in his face, and that Romulus was looking at him askance. "Of what are you disapproving my friend, scourging?"

"Forgive me sir, I had not meant to be disrespectful. It's just that I find it distasteful to strip a man of his dignity and abuse him when he has no defense of his own. It's one thing to face an equal in battle; it's another to take advantage of him when he's down. That is just the way I feel. Please forgive me if I have offended you by being so bold in my speech." The centurion continued looking at Articus with a jaundiced eye for a few moments, then seemed to relax some as he poured himself another drink from the pitcher on the tray.

"I wish I still could embrace the principles you proclaim so boldly and worthily my young friend, but I am afraid that time and the pressures of my job have caused me to compromise far more than I'd like to admit. When I was your age, I also envisioned myself as a man of honor and principle. There are many privileges of being a man under authority, for it gives one the ability to carry out many critical tasks denied to others. It also means those in authority over us can command us to do things we may not approve of or believe in. While there are occasions which cause me to suffer pangs of guilt for certain behavior, the fact remains that we are what we are, and I must forever live with some shortcomings in my life.

"Shall I continue my story?"

Articus relaxed a bit in his comfortable chair and said, "Please do sir, I am very interested in your account."

Notes

1. "Standing in the dock" is an idiomatic expression that means someone is being subjected to examination or trial.
2. Matthew 27:11
3. Matthew 27:19
4. Matthew 27:17
5. Matthew 27:21–26
6. A cohort consisted of 480 soldiers.
7. A conturbenium was a group of eight soldiers tightly bound together as a unit.
8. Matthew 27:27–31

CHAPTER
23

THE CRUCIFIXION

"About the ninth hour Jesus cried out with a loud voice saying, 'ELI, ELI, LAMA SABACHTHANI!, that is, 'My God, My God, why have You forsaken Me?'"

Acts 27:46

"As we prepared for our journey to Golgotha[1] I felt my elite *conturbenium* was as large a group as needed. It's only a short walk, about seventeen Stadia,[2] and the Jewish carpenter was too weak to attempt an escape, his supporters were mostly women and few in number, and the rest of the crowd supported his death.

"The path we took is used so often in escorting prisoners to their execution that the Jews have even given it a name, the 'Via Dolorosa.'[3] There were many gawkers along the way, and since *Yeshua* was in such bad shape, I pulled one man out of the crowd to help carry his cross. Since you've never seen a crucifixion, Articus, you may not realize the cross is in two pieces. The horizontal piece is strapped to the victim's shoulders with the longer, vertical piece affixed to it. We stopped, loosed the two poles, and gave the longer, heavier one to my "volunteer!" Turns out he had two sons with him, but they appeared old enough to take care of themselves until we got to Golgotha.[4]

"While you're here in Jerusalem you may hear two names for the hill where we crucified *Yeshua*: 'Golgotha,' which originates from Aramaic, and 'Calvaria,' which is Latin. Both come from the fact that it roughly resembles a human skull or cranium. Frankly, it is such an ugly place littered with human bones and skulls that it gives me the creeps just thinking about it! Because most of those put to death there are criminals and other rejects from society, few of their bodies ever receive a proper burial, even in a Potter's Field.[5] It is not uncommon to find remains just thrown into pits or shallow graves after hanging on the crosses for a time. Some bodies remain for weeks decomposing until nothing is left but the bones. Golgotha is not a pleasant place to visit, but it's very public location does send a message that Rome means business when it comes to the law.

"The walk to Golgotha following *Yeshua's* trial and scourging brought him pretty close to death's door. To keep him from going into shock and to make sure he lived long enough to receive the punishment for his crimes, we offered him a mild anesthetic of gall[6] mixed with wine. Never had I seen a condemned man refuse to ease his pain with a bit of spirits, but *Yeshua* flatly refused to take more than a sip."

Inwardly, Artie recoiled as he imagined the agony *Yeshua* would have endured. Though he never had been part of a crucifixion team, he certainly had seen the sickening results. More than once, he had walked on roads lined with crosses from which hung the rotting, mutilated corpses of those who had felt the harsh justice of Roman law (though Roman citizens themselves were exempt from the cruelty of crucifixion). As for himself, he found the practice of crucifixion to be barbaric and inhumane, and he couldn't help but wonder how a centurion like Romulus could have such a callous view of death.

THE CRUCIFIXION

Romulus continued...

"There were two other scheduled executions held that day, but the primary focus of the crowd was on the Jewish "Messiah" whom all those fanatics from the synagogue were raving about. They were merciless in their abuse, cursing him one minute and then mocking him for saying that he was a king. They were especially angry because Pilate had us put a sign on his cross above him that said, '*This is Yeshua, the King of the Jews.*' Many in the crowd were yelling, saying that if he really was *Yahweh* he should save himself and just come down from the cross. What they did was cruelty in its worst form. There was *Yeshua* hanging naked on the cross—bleeding, beaten almost beyond recognition[7] and totally helpless—with the rabble adding insult to injury by mocking him, spitting at him, and hurling the most despicable form of insults. Even one of the other prisoners hanging next to him was joining in the attacks.

"When it came to my own men, I should have exercised more discipline. I could have stopped them when they started dividing up *Yeshua's* clothing, but I didn't. I think I was just worn out from the long night and day I'd already been through, and just wasn't thinking clearly. *Yeshua* did have friends and relatives present, and they were entitled to his belongings. At least my soldiers had sense enough not to tear his seamless tunic into pieces but cast lots for it. Like yours, their uniforms are free, but they have to buy their own civilian clothes. As you've experienced at your own pay grade, you take advantage of anything you can get for free.

"As I said, one of the prisoners hanging on a cross next to *Yeshua's* cursed him viciously, but the other seemed to think

Yeshua might really be *Yahweh* and did the strangest thing! First, he rebuked the first criminal for what he was doing and said: '*We are suffering justly and receiving what we deserve for our deeds; but this man has done nothing wrong.*' Then he turned to *Yeshua*, asking that he remember him when *Yeshua* came into his kingdom. At that request, *Yeshua* told him, '*Truly I say to you, today you shall be with Me in Paradise.*'[8] For some reason, that exchange really shook me up! If a hardened criminal like that could recognize the wrong in his own life, and in the short time he'd been near *Yeshua* on the cross could sense something other-worldly about him, what clue had I missed in all the time I'd spent with him the past twenty-four hours? His mother also was standing near the cross with some of his followers, and he asked one of them to look after her as if he were her son.[9] How *Yeshua* could be so kind when he was in such pain and near death was just about beyond belief! My head was spinning while I tried to process all this. It was about noon, and I was beginning to think part of my problem was hunger, so I told myself 'I need food!' Then things happened so rapidly I totally forgot about being hungry.

"First the sun was obscured, and darkness fell over the entire land for about three hours. We hadn't brought torches because it had been full daylight, but we sure needed them then. That in itself gave the entire landscape an eerie, ghostly feeling. Then about three o'clock, *Yeshua* called out with a loud voice, '*ELI, ELI, LAMA SABACHTHANI?*'[10] Some of the bystanders thought he was calling for a prophet called Elijah. One of them filled a sponge with sour wine and held it up to him on a stick, but the others called out, 'Wait! Let's see if Elijah will really come to save him!'[11]

"Next came an action we Romans didn't understand until it was explained by knowledgeable Jewish scholars. Articus, unless you've studied the Jewish religion you may not know that the most sacred inner portion of their temple is 'off limits' to all but a few privileged members of the Jewish priestly class. It is so sacred that Rome has made it very clear we cannot go beyond the outer courtyards. That inner portion is divided into two halls with a heavy veil separating them, with the innermost one called 'The Holy of Holies.' No one may enter into it except the Jewish High Priest and then only once a year on the day they call 'The Atonement.' When I say 'No One!' I mean 'No One!' Rumor has it that when the High Priest goes in on that special day, they even tie a rope around his ankle in case he dies while inside. Then they can pull his body out instead of leaving it to decay for a year until the next Day of Atonement. Weird people those Jews!

"What happened after the sky turned black is unbelievable: that heavy veil was torn in two from top to bottom! Articus, it is fifty feet from floor to ceiling in the temple. No human could have torn that veil in two from the top down without being on a very tall scaffolding. It was as though it was torn apart by the Hand of God reaching down from heaven! Those priests who saw it happen must have been scared out of their wits! I bet it made some of them wonder if they should have believed *Yeshua* when he said he was the Son of *Yahweh*! Then there was a violent earthquake that shook the earth and split rocks open. But the most frightening part to me was when tombs opened up, and some of *Yeshua's* followers who had died came out of them to go into Jerusalem where they were seen by many. Son, I normally don't believe in ghosts, but I sure did that day!

"People were screaming, running, and falling down, and my men were as frightened as the crowd, wanting me to tell them what to do. Frankly, I was too dumbfounded to say or do anything. It was as though *Yeshua* had been on a great mission which had been completed, and he was free to leave. In fact, he seemed to dismiss his spirit and walk away from life on his own choosing. He basically controlled the moment of his death. I have seen a lot of men die, but none ever died like that man.

"I was so frightened at that point I cried out, '*Truly this man was the Son of Yahweh.*' I wasn't the only one who came to that conclusion. So did my soldiers and some of the civilians who were present.[12] I even heard later that some Jews who were present became followers of *Yeshua* later. His demeanor, the unexplained darkness, earthquake, and other phenomena of that day are what swayed me. But I heard what made the greatest impression on the Jews was when that thick, heavy, tightly woven veil in their temple was torn in two from top to bottom. It was meant to hide from public view the place where the Jews claim *Yahweh* dwelt. With it in tatters, some present felt it was a sure sign that *Yeshua* was their *Messiah*. Some claim that the death of *Yeshua* was some sort of atonement for their sins, giving them free entry into heaven when they died. For me, after thinking it over I had to conclude this man either was a lunatic or exactly who he said he was. But from what I experienced all the time I was with him, I have to tell you right out—he was no lunatic!"

Artie was fascinated by what he heard. He thought: "Is it possible there really is one supreme god who cares so much about all humans who have been born on this earth that he became a man like other men and walked among us? Is such a thing even possible?" It was truly hard to believe.

A strange kind of hunger and thirst welled up within Artie, a deep desire to have known *Yeshua* while he was alive. Then he could have talked with him as a man talks to a friend and discovered from firsthand experience if he really is the Son of *Yahweh*. Artie wondered why he felt that way? It was as though a voice somewhere in his heart and head were telling him that in *Yeshua* could be found the deepest answers to the oldest questions of life: *Who am I? Why am I here? Where am I going when I die?* Why could he not have met *Yeshua* while he was still alive? If he had, maybe all those questions would have been answered. But with *Yeshua's* death, he never would have that opportunity. Why had Cornelius sent him to Romulus for answers to his questions since Romulus's experience with *Yeshua* ended with his death?

Snapping out of his musing, Artie questioned Romulus, "Is he really dead?"

Notes

1. Also called the Hill of Calvary.
2. About two miles.
3. Meaning "Sorrowful Way" or "Way of Suffering."
4. Mark 15:21
5. A place of burial for unknown, unclaimed, or indigent people.
6. Gall most often refers to a bitter-tasting substance made of a plant such as wormwood or myrrh.
7. Isaiah 52:13–15
8. Luke 23:39–43
9. John 19:25–27
10. Matthew 27:46—"My God, My God, why hast Thou forsaken Me?"
11. Matthew 27:45–49
12. Matthew 27:54

CHAPTER
24

THE END...OR THE BEGINNING?

Joseph of Arimathea laid Yeshua's body in his own new tomb and rolled a large stone against the entrance of the tomb.[1]

"A severe earthquake occurred, an angel of the Lord descended from heaven and came and rolled away the stone and sat upon it."

Matthew 28:2

"Dead, you ask? He's as dead as all whose bones which lie rotting about the grounds of Golgotha," quipped Romulus. "Because it was getting late and the Sabbath was upon us, the Jewish leaders wanted to make certain the three men's bodies would not remain on their crosses overnight. So, they went to Pilate and asked for their legs to be broken. My men broke the legs of the two crucified on either side of *Yeshua* but found that the carpenter was already dead. When one of my men pierced his side with a spear, immediately blood and water came out. I was there and could affirm to the Governor that *Yeshua* was dead. So, was he dead? Of course, he was!

"Where was I? Oh yes, one of the Jewish leaders apparently didn't agree with what the rest of the Sanhedrin did, so he asked permission from the Governor to take away the body of *Yeshua*, which Pilate gave. I was grateful for his action, as my men and I were worn out from the ordeal and ready to return to the garrison and stiff drinks! I don't know what happened to the other two who died but suspect their bones may still be at Golgotha.

"I thought that would be the end of the story, but it was not.

"The day after the Jewish preparation day, the Chief Priests and Pharisees went back to Pilate asking for the tomb to be guarded and a seal placed on the stone. They remembered that when *Yeshua* was still alive he had said that, 'After three days I will rise again.'[2] I don't know what their problem was. If they thought he had the power to raise himself from the dead, why didn't they listen to his message and just 'get in step' with him? They covered their actions by saying it was because they thought his followers would try to steal his body, but that didn't make any sense! Who would want to steal a decaying corpse from a perfectly good tomb? I think they were just born troublemakers trying to prove they were somebody! At any rate, the Governor gave in to their whining and said, 'Alright, I will give you your guard for three days,' and he called on us again.[3] So I authorized three groups of soldiers to stay on guard duty, rotating 'round-the-clock' for the next three days.

"Everything went as scheduled until Sunday morning. No one bothered the tomb, and my men just played cards and enjoyed getting out of the normal Saturday inspection of their barracks. But Sunday morning was something else!

"Earthquakes aren't unusual in this part of Israel, but two big ones close together rarely happen. After the quake the day we crucified *Yeshua*, no one expected another one to happen on Sunday, but it did. Then my soldiers on duty said an angel came down from heaven and rolled the stone away. At that point, their military training 'went out the window,' and they became like dead men. Some of the women who were *Yeshua's* followers were also there, and the angel told them, '*Don't be afraid; for I know you are looking for Yeshua who has been crucified. He is not here, for He is risen, just as He said. Come, see the place where he was lying!*'[4] I don't know what the women did, but my guys high-tailed it back into town. If they could run that fast all the time, I'd assign them as long-distance couriers!

"What my officers did next was completely out of protocol. Instead of reporting to me what had happened, they went to the Chief Priests and told them. In my debriefing afterwards I discovered that the priests had given them a large sum of money and told them to say, '*His Disciples came by night and stole Him away while we were asleep.*'[5] Their actions placed both them and me in a lot of trouble with my high command. If they did fall asleep, my usual punishment would simply be to throw them in the brig for a few days. But as you know, taking a bribe is a serious offense that could lead to flogging, imprisonment, or even death. If I accuse the Jewish leadership of bribery to get my soldiers to lie, I am in trouble both with them and with Rome. My boy, never think for one minute that becoming a centurion will solve all your problems. As the old saying goes, 'The closer you get to the sun, the easier it is to get burned.' Even with the time that has passed since his crucifixion, the higher-ups are still trying to figure out how to handle the matter. I suspect whatever they decide it won't go that well for me. When you put that together with the fact that I oversaw the execution of *Yeshua*, sometimes I think my life isn't worth half a shekel. If he was the Son of *Yahweh* as I said the day we crucified him, I can never forgive myself for my part in his death. If he wasn't, how can I explain what I exclaimed that day as well as the actions of my men who said they saw an angel that Sunday morning?

"Artie, I have told you all I know about the whole matter. From what I saw and heard that extraordinary weekend is beyond comprehension. There is no question but that *Yeshua* was not an ordinary man; I don't really know who he was or is. I would like to believe he is who he said he is, and that maybe even a tough hardened old warrior like me could be accepted into his kingdom. There are many things in my life for which I am ashamed, and it gives me comfort to think someone could look me in the eye and say: 'You are forgiven of all your bad deeds.' I am told that *Yeshua* spoke often on peace, love, forgiveness, and a home in heaven. Maybe at my age I'm too old, too guilty, or just too far gone even to think of having those things. But if not, the peace he offered certainly would help calm my spirit now!"

With those remarks, Romulus rose from his chair, signaling to Artie their meeting had ended. Artie quickly stood, thanking the centurion for his hospitality and his candor in his recollections about *Yeshua*. After retrieving his helmet and cloak from Romulus's office, Artie again thanked his host for the gracious refreshments and willingness to discuss with him such a painful subject.

Before Artie could leave his presence, Romulus offered one concluding thought: "I truly hope you find answers to the questions you are seeking."

Stepping into the outer courtyard, Artie encountered the same servant who had ushered him in to see Romulus, staring intently at Artie with an unwavering gaze. It was highly unusual for a servant to make strong eye contact with a superior, certainly not a sign of humility and respect. It was as if the man was trying to communicate something important to him. Though the stare lasted but a few seconds, it was long enough for Artie to take notice. Then the moment passed, and Artie was on his way.

Notes

1. Matthew 27:59–60
2. Mark 9:31
3. Matthew 27:62–66
4. Matthew 28:2–6
5. Matthew 28:13

CHAPTER
25

CLAUDIUS

"You grew weary in your search, but you never gave up. Desire gave you renewed strength, and you did not grow weary."

Isaiah 57:10

The streets of Jerusalem were greatly in need of repair. Potholes of assorted sizes and descriptions were the rule rather than the exception. Here and there, attempts had been made to fill in some of the holes with loose stones and sand, but most of the cavities lay naked and waiting for a misplaced foot or the wheel of an unsuspecting vendor's cart.

The city was not as impressive as Artie had expected, but it did have a distinct flavor of "Old World" charm and historical significance. Though the massive walls of Old Jerusalem bore the scars of countless attacks over the centuries, they still stood as a symbol of Jewish pride and religious patriotism. Artie found himself drawn to the famous temple of the Jews. It was indeed a magnificent sight, looming larger than life in the heart of the city. A brilliant afternoon sun shone brightly against the massive stone columns, highlighting the attention which had been given to ornate details in the carvings and bas-relief of the structure—workmanship which rivaled that of similarly spectacular edifices in Rome.

Artie wandered aimlessly about, not giving much thought as to where he was headed. Sooner or later, he should get on the road to Caesarea, but since he wasn't due there for a couple of days, he was in no real hurry to return. Certainly, what he had seen and heard the last few days had impacted his life, and he just needed time to think about it. He puzzled over the possibility his own father may have been a member of "The Way." More than ever, he wished they could have talked together face-to-face and that his father was still alive to counsel him. Though they had never met as adults, Artie had a deep sense of longing for the relationship of a father and a son.

Artie soon found himself in the marketplace, bustling with afternoon shoppers. He stopped at the stall of an aging fishmonger hawking fresh smoked fish seasoned with leeks, onions, and assorted herbs, wrapped in steamed kale. After a few casual comments, he asked about the fish. The old man offered him a sample, boasting that the Governor himself had tasted it and liked it so well he'd often send his personal chef to get some for his dinner table. "It's my own secret creation, the best in Jerusalem if I say so myself!"

Now that he had a captive audience, the fishmonger began to lament about poor sales and high taxes, and what the world was coming to. As he launched into his tirade, Artie thought to himself, *Looks like this fellow and Romulus went to the same "school of complaints!" All they can talk about is how the youth of today have it so good and how much harder life was when they were growing up.*

Savoring the sample offered him, Artie didn't know if it was the finest in Jerusalem, but he did know he wanted more! So, he placed his order, which included a bite of bread and some fresh herbs as well as an extra piece of fish wrapped in some kind of leaves to eat on the journey home. With care he tore the hot fish into pieces, licking his fingers after each flaky bite to make certain he didn't lose any of the rich seasoned sauce. Even though the extra piece would be cold when he ate it later, perhaps he might spot an out-of-the-way place to camp out, build a small campfire to warm both it and him, enjoy a bottle of wine and drink in the majesty of the night sky. He thought that might be preferable to paying the cost of an inn and putting up with other travelers. Besides, he needed the solitude to meditate on his own thoughts.

Breaking into his thoughts, the old fishmonger spoke: "Are you aware you are being followed?" Turning from his eating, Artie saw the servant of Romulus who had made such strong eye contact with him as he was leaving the centurion's office.

"Can we talk, Master?" spoke the servant. This time, the man's eyes were averted in acknowledgement of the rank and position of the Roman officer.

"Talk about what?" questioned Artie.

"About The Way," responded the servant.

"Speak," said Artie.

"My name is Claudius. As you know, I am a servant to Romulus. I won't take but a moment of your time, sir, but I have information which may help in your search for truth about *Yeshua* of Nazareth. Perhaps we could step over here out of the way?"

Artie looked around to see if others appeared interested in their conversation. However, since everyone around seemed to be focused on their own agenda, Artie quickly finished his food and gestured for the servant to follow him. A short walk led to an arched doorway that seemed to give the privacy needed for their conversation.

"What do you have to tell me? Are you a member of The Way?"

"Yes, and I can take you to someone who knows Him quite well. He can tell you many things about *Yeshua* gleaned from a very close personal relationship with Him."

"Does Romulus know this man, or is he aware you have followed me?"

"No sir, I am doing this on my own. I've observed how desperately you want to learn about *Yeshua*, and I can take you to a man who is his close friend."

"You mean WAS his close friend; *Yeshua* is dead! Your master, Romulus, personally saw to his crucifixion on orders from the Governor himself, Pontius Pilate!"

Once again, looking Artie straight in the eyes, the servant responded: "Not so my lord, He is alive! The man I can take you to has walked and talked with *Yeshua* since the crucifixion. He actually has touched his living body and can vouch for the fact that he is alive. *Yeshua* lives, he is not an apparition!"

Studying the servant's face, Artie could see the man indeed was very serious and totally believed what he spoke was true.

"Your master Romulus did not speak of such a person to me, why are you?"

Still looking boldly into Artie's eyes, Claudius continued. "My master, Romulus, does not know the man of whom I speak. I am not sure where my master stands concerning The Way, so I have hesitated to speak much about it. But you are different. I sense you have a sincere desire to know the truth, and I feel the *Spirit of Yeshua* would have me share the truth with you. Please believe me when I say no harm will come to you in meeting this man. He is a friend, and I believe you will be much the wiser after you meet with him."

Artie studied the face of the man before him. Claudius did not have the look of a deceiver, and he felt he could trust him. He appeared to be about his same age and build, but Artie felt because of his military training he could overpower Claudius if anything went wrong.

"Alright, I will accompany you. However, if I sense treachery afoot you will feel the chill of death from the blade of my dagger. Do we understand each other?"

"Yes sir, I know you will not regret your decision to meet with this man. Like you, at one time he too was a doubter. But when confronted by *Yeshua* himself, all he could do was fall on his knees and exclaim, '*My Lord and my God!*'"[1]

Notes

1. John 20:28

CHAPTER
26

THOMAS

"One of the twelve disciples, Thomas (nicknamed the Twin) was not with the others when Jesus came. They told him, 'We have seen the Lord!' But he replied, 'I won't believe it unless I see the nail wounds in his hands, put my fingers into them, and place my hand into the wound in his side.'"

John 20:24–25

Twenty-minutes later, both men passed by the Jaffa Gate on the road to the Washerman's Field and entered a side street off the main road. Small square doorways lined both sides of the narrow street, attached to dwellings which appeared to be centuries old and typical of a working-class neighborhood. The few people stirring about in the early afternoon heat gave curious glances at the sight of a Roman officer being led by a member of the Jewish working class, and several stopped dead in their tracks for a little rubbernecking. Most were older men who still counted the Roman presence as an unwanted intrusion into the Jewish way of life.

Artie took note of the stares, well aware of the underlying hostility toward the Roman occupiers. He suspected he might feel the same way if another nation was occupying his own country. Still, *to the victor belongs the spoils,* he thought, *and as an loyal officer of Rome I have duties to perform. Besides,* he told himself, *since I and my fellow officers are responsible for the protection and security of ALL the people of the region—both Jews and Romans—we are providing them a service as well. They should be grateful that they are enjoying the protection of Rome rather than enduring the harsh rule of some of the hostile tribes and rulers of the region.*

About halfway down the narrow street, Claudius stopped in front of a rather large and ornate door which seemed to be a beacon among the many others. Masterfully carved into its wood was the image of an olive tree, its branches radiating outward from a thick trunk chiseled into the hard wood with great attention to every detail. The leaves displayed intricate patterns of veins rich in texture, and the olives hanging by their stems appeared to be real enough to reach out and pluck. The artistry was the handywork of a master wood carver. "This is the place!" declared Claudius! Striking the heel of his hand against the door in three sharp raps, Claudius bent a listening ear for the sound of movement within.

Out of habit and training, Artie stepped to one side of the door and pressed his frame closer to the wall of the dwelling. He had taught himself never to be taken by surprise with what/who might be on the other side of a door. As a precaution against any who hoped to catch him off-guard, unconsciously he moved his hand to the handle of his weapon.

Once again, Claudius gave a sound rap to the door, this time with more force. Several moments passed, but before he could rap on the door again the sound of movement inside was heard distinctly. Then a soft feminine voice from within inquired in Hebrew as to who might be at the door. Glancing at Artie, Claudius replied in Greek, knowing that the officer would not be comfortable if the others conversed in Hebrew.

"Claudius Bar-Helek,[1] to see my friend, Thomas."

A bolt slid open, and a small "peep-hole" door in the larger door opened slightly, allowing the person inside to see who was outside. From the sound of the voice and what Artie could see of the speaker, it appeared to be a young woman. When she recognized Claudius, a smile danced across her face, and her tone of voice brightened. As she cracked open the large door and Artie could see her more clearly, he recognized she was the captivating young woman from whom he had bought the lamp in Caesarea a few days ago. However, she did not recognize him at first, seeing only a dreaded Roman officer, and her smile quickly faded. Noting her change in demeanor, Claudius spoke quickly in hopes of neutralizing her concerns: "Have no fear, Abigail. This officer is here as a friend and not on official business for Rome. Now, please take us to your brother Thomas without delay."

Hesitating for only a moment longer, Abigail opened the door sufficiently to allow the two men to enter. Simultaneously she quickly reached with her free hand to cover the bridge of her nose with her veil, thereby obscuring all but her eyes to this stranger in her midst. Even though she moved quickly, Artie still had time for a good look at the beautiful face he had seen in the market, a face he had thought he would never see again.

Her eyes were what disarmed him. They were of the color of brilliant jade and were so penetrating that his knees went weak, and he felt defenseless in her presence. He was further transfixed by hair as black as a raven's and skin the color of dark, smooth olives. Recalling his first fleeting glance at her lovely face, this new glimpse had it fixed in his mind forever. Her lips were delicate and the color of scarlet ribbon, and her teeth as white as new fallen snow. She was slim with graceful small hands and feet, and Artie imagined what it would be like to fasten a finely filigreed gold chain around her slender neck. He was smitten! He felt a warm glow pass over his entire body and had an aching sense of longing to hold her close to him. It was as if he had been searching for her his whole life and now that he had found her, needed to know so much more—NOW! Though he didn't know it then, Artie was not alone in sensing the awakening of love; Abigail had noticed the handsome young officer and felt a fluttering in her breast. Before shyly averting her eyes, she had seen just enough of him that her imagination already was at work.

As the two men followed the girl inside, Artie's mind remained focused on this picture of loveliness. He thought he caught just a subtle hint of jasmine in the air. "It must be what she is wearing," he thought. Jasmine was a popular fragrance throughout the region, so Artie was familiar with its scent. He had often wondered how such a beautiful flower could be part of the olive tree *genus*, and how it could be made either into a perfume or a delicate tea. What he did know, however, is that from that day forward, the fragrance of jasmine would forever be associated with this beautiful maiden.

Once inside the house, the two men waited in a small foyer while Abigail excused herself to get her brother. Though most of her face was covered with her veil, Artie couldn't help but notice she gave him another furtive glance and was blushing a little as she left.

Regaining his composure, Artie made a visual inventory of the small foyer, which served as an anteroom for visitors awaiting formal introductions to the head of the home. Such a room denoted a family of some means or social status and generally was not found in the more common households of the region.

There were no chairs or sitting areas in the room, but there were several wooden pegs affixed to the walls where cloaks, bags, or belted weapons could be hung. Of particular interest was a cloak of purple cloth hanging from one of the pegs and a woolen carpet which graced the stone floor. The only other furnishings were two large clay jugs of unequal size of the type used to haul water and an unlit oil lamp sitting in a niche in the brick and mud plaster wall. Artie remembered that when he had purchased the oil lamp from Abigail, she said she often helped make them with her own hands. *I wonder if she made this one?* he pondered. Light for the room came from several rectangular windows located above the doorway and along the outer wall. Each was approximately two feet long and about six inches high. They were enough to allow entry of sunlight and the exchange of fresh air but small enough to prohibit intruders.

Artie's thoughts were cut short when he heard a man's strong voice boom out "Hello Claudius, my friend! So good to see you. Please come in." He and Claudius each turned to face the man who had just entered the room. The young soldier was disappointed that Abigail had not returned with her brother, but his senses were heightened with the hope this man could shed more light on his quest to know about *Yeshua*.

The speaker appeared to be in his early to mid-thirties with brownish-red hair and a short beard of equal color. He was shorter than either Artie or Claudius and had the weathered look of a man who had traveled many miles by foot and knew how to take care of himself. His smile was genuine and his manner easy, but his brown eyes expressed cautiousness and deep thought. He spoke directly to Claudius, but his eyes never left Artie.

Sensing the nervousness of his friend and the edge in his voice, Claudius got right to the point: "Thomas, may I introduce you to Articus Maximus, a man who, I believe, seeks truth with regard to our Lord, *Yeshua*. He made the journey here from his post in Caesarea to meet with Romulus, hoping to learn more. Though Romulus was able to give him detailed information about the trials and crucifixion of *Yeshua*, Romulus does not have true understanding of who *Yeshua* is or why He had to die on the cross. Overhearing their conversation, I know this young soldier truly wants a deeper understanding of why *Yeshua* came to earth. He has a sincere interest in why His followers believe *Yeshua* is *Yahweh* in the flesh, and why they have come together in The Way to explain that message to others.

Claudius spent the better part of the next five to ten minutes giving Thomas many details of the conversation between Artie and Romulus. As Artie listened, it became evident that while it had seemed Romulus and he were alone in their meeting earlier that day, others were eavesdropping from some hidden recess of the portico. No wonder the servant looked so intently at him as he left his meeting with the centurion. After explaining that he had followed Artie to the fishmonger's hoping to bring him to meet Thomas, Claudius formally introduced the two men.

Once he comprehended the purpose of the visit, Thomas began to speak…

"Officer, I know there is little friendship and love between the Jews and Roman occupiers, but please know you are an honored guest in my home. I consider it a privilege for us to sit together and talk of things I believe can help bridge the gap between you and us." Acknowledging Thomas's offer of friendship and information, Artie thanked him and then followed him and Claudius through a curtained doorway into a second room.

That room was quite sizable and bathed in natural light from a small private courtyard. Tastefully decorated, it contained several handmade carpets covering the stone floor and a couple of low couches, piled high with pillows of goatskin stuffed with sheep's wool. Three water jars, not unlike the ones found in the anteroom, stood in one corner, and several wineskins hung from cords of leather looped over pegs in the wall. A square table, perched on short legs approximately a foot off the floor, was the centerpiece of the room. On its surface were several bowls filled with melons, figs, pomegranates, apricots, and some type of dried citrus fruit. A plate containing what appeared to be a fresh loaf of bread covered by a linen cloth completed the table setting.

In the courtyard, twin columns held up an overhanging roof structure constructed of woven matting. Though technically not a roof, the covering served as an awning for shade and gave some protection from inclement weather. Longer than it was wide, the courtyard contained two date palms in its center surrounded by variegated shrubbery of some kind. With green outer leaves tipped in shades of yellow, the shrubs lent a pleasant accent to the courtyard's plantings. Generous clusters of ripe dates hung from the giant pods of the fruiting palms; their rich sweet sticky nectar attested to by the number of bees swarming about the ripened fruit.

Always on the alert, the policeman in him caused Artie to notice several doorways on the opposite side of the courtyard. These probably led to sleeping quarters for the occupants of the household. Overall, it was a warm and inviting Jewish home, built originally for the more affluent but now located in a more working-class section of the old city.

"May I offer either of you something to eat?" asked Thomas, gesturing to the fruit and bread. Both men answered "No." Artie said he'd just eaten, and Claudius explained that he really needed to return home, for Romulus would be expecting him soon. "In fact," he said, "I already have been away too long. He thinks I am at the market picking up some things for a dinner party to be held at his home this evening, and I must not be late in my return."

Turning to Artie, Claudius said: "I leave you in good hands, sir. It is my sincere desire that you find answers to the questions you have about The Way. I hope my bringing you to Thomas will have played even some minor part in your finding the truth about life." With that, Claudius extended his right hand and forearm to Artie in a gesture of greeting and farewell customary among the Romans. Somewhat taken aback, Artie hesitated at first, then extended his own right hand and forearm, grasping the forearm of Claudius in the traditional Roman recognition of friendship. Inwardly, Artie pondered what he had done. *What would Cornelius think if he knew I'd acknowledged friendship with a Jew? What about my friends? Is this something I should have done? Will it be expected from me in the future, even when I leave this man's home?* Thomas interrupted those thoughts by offering him a comfortable place where the two could converse easily. Then he began with the most incredible account concerning *Yeshua* that Artie ever could have imagined!

Notes

1. "Bar" is Aramaic for "son of."

CHAPTER

27

CALLED BY *YESHUA*

"It was at this time that Jesus went off to the mountain to pray, and He spent the whole night in prayer to God. And when day came, He called His disciples to Him and chose twelve of them, whom He also named as apostles."

Luke 6:12–13

"Where do I begin?" Thomas mused, speaking mainly to himself. Claudius's departure a few moments earlier prompted Thomas to share his compelling personal account. "I suppose I should begin by telling you that I was one of the twelve men *Yeshua* asked to become members of His inner group, men who would spend three years closely in His presence, getting to know Him as well as it is possible to know another person. We traveled with Him through all kinds of weather, slept at night wherever we found accommodations, often out under the stars. We ate the same food as He, heard all His public messages, discoursed privately with Him for hours on end, and questioned Him extensively on Jewish history and the many prophecies written in the Jewish scrolls. Though many others accepted His teachings and followed Him over the three years of His public ministry, we twelve were the handpicked core group *Yeshua* poured Himself into. He ordained us to become apostles after His death, the first of many who would take His message of salvation to all mankind, both Jews and Gentiles.

"I long have been a student of the *Torah*[1] and of the writings and traditions of the Jewish prophets, especially as relates to the expected *Messiah*. In spite of my background in those matters, I am not sure why the Lord selected me as one of His disciples. But I will be forever grateful He looked beyond my faults to include me as one of His close associates.

"It was John the baptizer who first captured my attention with his message of repentance. Like many others I knew that as a nation we had drifted far from *Yahweh's* commands and had suffered greatly for all our sins. When John began preaching in the Judean wilderness saying '*Repent, for the kingdom of heaven is near,*'[2] I was electrified by the urgency of his message and his tone of voice. I thought of what the prophet Isaiah had prophesied: '*The voice of one crying in the wilderness, make ready the way of Yeshua, make His paths straight!,*'[3] and I couldn't help but wonder if John was the one '*crying in the wilderness*' and *Yeshua* the one who would usher in the kingdom of heaven. Then I was there the day *Yeshua* came to the River Jordan and asked John to baptize Him. At first John refused, saying he needed to be baptized by *Yeshua*. Even so, he complied with *Yeshua's* request saying, '*Behold the Lamb of Yahweh who takes away the sins of the world.*'[4] Just as the baptism took place I saw *Yahweh's Spirit* descend like a dove upon *Yeshua* and heard a voice from heaven say '*This is My beloved Son in whom I am well-pleased.*'[5] As all this slowly sunk in, I began to see *Yeshua* in the light of many prophetic words concerning the *Messiah*. I was mesmerized by *Yeshua* and wanted to know as much about Him and His mission as was humanly possible. After He called me to join His inner circle and I began to know Him more closely, I realized He was not just an ordinary man. As Romulus said at the time of His crucifixion, I came to know that *'Surely this man is the Son of Yahweh!'*

"Many of those who listened to His messages and felt their power were convinced *Yeshua* was the promised *Messiah* who had come in fulfillment of a prophecy made by our father Jacob (also called Israel). He had said that out of Judah would come a lion with a scepter and a *'ruler's staff between his feet.'*[6] Some of His followers believed that under *Yeshua's* leadership they would grow strong enough to free Israel from foreign domination and rule, and that *Yeshua* would be king. They missed the truth uttered by John when he said, *'Behold the Lamb of Yahweh who takes away the sins of the world.'* For just as the ancient prophets had said there would come a time when *Yeshua* would be King, the prophet Isaiah clarified that He first would come as a sacrificial lamb to pay for the sins of *all* mankind.[7] I admit, young officer, there were times when I had the same misunderstanding. But in time I came to understand that only after becoming that 'lamb' would *Yeshua* become 'the Lion of Judah.' When we asked *Yeshua* when that time would be, He said only *Yahweh* knew the day and the hour.[8] It wasn't until after all the miracles He performed, His teaching, His death, and His resurrection that we finally began to grasp the full significance of what the prophets had been saying since the very beginning of man's history on earth.

"I don't know what you believe or have been told concerning *Yeshua*, and it is not my desire to school you in Jewish history concerning the prophets of old or of the promised *Messiah*; I will leave that to others. What I will say is that after *Yeshua* was taken into custody and was tried unjustly as Romulus told you, was crucified and buried, He did return to life. It is my understanding that Romulus also told you that *Yeshua* died on the cross, was buried in a sealed tomb, that some of his own soldiers saw an angel roll back the stone, and that the tomb was empty. We both agree on those facts, but I had the additional joy in the weeks after He rose from that tomb to walk with Him, talk with Him, share a meal with Him, and finally understand that His voluntary death was a gift to all mankind in payment for my sins and yours. Though this may be hard for you to comprehend, I know for a fact that He is alive and truly is the *Son* of *Yahweh*. In time I hope you can come to this same level of understanding. A moment ago, I mentioned the Jewish prophet, Isaiah. He wrote: '*How lovely on the mountains are the feet of him who brings good news, who announces peace and brings good news of happiness, who announces salvation and says to Zion, Yahweh reigns.*'[9] Articus, my feet aren't very lovely! But I have just 'announced to you' the Good News about *Yeshua*, who has brought salvation to Israel and all mankind. My prayer is that through the power of His *Holy Spirit*, *Yahweh* will open your heart and mind to the truth you have now heard."

At this juncture, Artie did not know what to think. Romulus told him that at the time of *Yeshua's* crucifixion he had declared that *Yeshua* was the Son of *Yahweh*, but now he wasn't sure. The soldiers guarding the tomb said an angel had rolled the stone away, but Romulus said they were bribed by Jewish leaders to say his body had been stolen. Now Thomas had told him another story—that he had extensive experience with a man who had been crucified yet still lives, and that man—*Yeshua*—actually was born to die and then come back to life for the benefit of all mankind. What and who should he believe? Is all what Thomas said really possible?

Thomas continued.

"The body of *Yeshua* was taken down from the cross and buried in a new tomb belonging to a member of the Sanhedrin, Joseph of Arimathea, who did not agree to His crucifixion. A high-ranking Pharisee named Nicodemus, also outraged at what had transpired, joined Joseph in preparing His body for burial.[10] Much to our everlasting shame, the eleven of us who had been His closest disciples fled after a disgraced member of our group, Judas (also known as Simon Iscariot) betrayed Him. We didn't know what to think. Our leader was dead, one of our close members was a traitor, and we wondered which of us might also be targeted to die. Our hopes and dreams for the restoration of Israel as an independent nation were over, and we all thought this was the end of what *Yeshua* had begun. I was in a state of depression and shock, and over the next few days I had a hard time eating, sleeping, or just functioning in general. I had lost my dearest friend, and life held no purpose for me.

"Imagine my surprise when I heard from some of the other disciples that *Yeshua* was alive. At first, I became enraged at such a preposterous idea, thinking their talk was a cruel joke. I already had heard that a woman we knew, Mary from the town of Magdala, claimed to have seen *Yeshua* near His tomb early Sunday morning. She had become a strong follower of

Yeshua after he healed her of a variety of problems, and I thought perhaps she was suffering from delusions or some other sort of problem.

"*Yeshua* was also said to have appeared to a man named Cleopas and his friend as they were walking the seven miles from Jerusalem to their home in Emmaus. Even though they had been His followers, they said they didn't recognize Him until after He went into their home for a meal with them. However, during their walk they said He spoke so knowledgeably and compassionately about what had happened, they hung on to His every word. Then, when he accepted their invitation to eat and blessed the meal, their eyes were opened to realize who He was. Then He vanished from their sight, 'into thin air' as you might say.[11] At that point they turned right back around and hurried back to Jerusalem to share what had happened. After that, *Yeshua* was seen by more and more individuals to the extent it was hard to believe that it could be any other but Him. Still, I personally had not seen Him and didn't want to accept at face value what others were saying."

"But did you see him, I mean ACTUALLY SEE HIM in person?" interrupted Artie. "That's what's important to me."

"Please be patient, young man, so I can finish my story. Not long after the news began to spread that *Yeshua* was alive, my opportunity came. Some of the other disciples told me He was alive, and that they had all seen Him. But I told them until I saw Him in person and touched Him myself, I could not believe the reports.

"Then eight days later we all were gathered for a meeting. The door to the room was locked for fear the Jewish leaders would barge in and arrest us. Suddenly, without warning, *Yeshua* was among us. One second, He was not there, the next He was. He just appeared out of nowhere. I checked the door and found it was still locked. Yeshua entered and left that room by His own supernatural power.[12]

"Almost immediately He approached me and said, '*Reach here with your finger, and see My hands; and reach here your hand and put it into My side; and do not be unbelieving, but believing.*' Immediately I knew it was Him, and I said, '*My Lord and my God!*'[13] Immediately I knew that what I had been hearing was true; *Yeshua* truly is alive! I was standing in a room with the Creator of all things.[14] There is no way to describe the sense of awe, wonderment, and joy I knew that instant and every minute since. He had accomplished what He said He would: die and be raised back to life, thereby paying for the sins of all mankind so everyone could have the opportunity to become sons of *Yahweh*.[15]

"Artie, I am certain you are a credit to your family and to the Roman government. But as diligently as you strive to lead an upright life, somewhere along the way you will make mistakes, perhaps to the detriment of yourself and others. In our ancient scrolls we Jews frequently find this statement, '*There is no one who does good, not even one.*'[16] That observation applies to all, whether Jew or Roman. But through the crucifixion and resurrection of *Yeshua*, *Yahweh* has offered forgiveness to each of us, whether Jew or Roman. Artie, *Yahweh* loves you and wants to have a personal relationship with you. For all who place their hope and trust in *Yeshua* and in the price He paid on the cross, He has promised His *Holy Spirit* will indwell us during this lifetime, and we will spend eternity in heaven with Him when our life on this earth is ended."

As Artie heard Thomas echoing what he had heard Peter speak, he realized how similar both were in their words and depth of their convictions. He had no doubt but that both men truly believed everything they had said concerning *Yeshua*. But it contrasted so sharply with what he had been taught about there being multiple gods and idols. Who was telling the truth, his former teachers or Peter and Thomas? Also, Artie knew that his life viewed in the teachings of *Yeshua* and the two apostles was filled with wrongs and shortcomings. Considering that, would *Yeshua* be willing to forgive him, and could he become a member of "The Way" even though he wasn't a Jew?

Sensing what was on Artie's mind, Thomas resumed speaking. "Young man, let me explain that what *Yahweh* and *Yeshua* did applies to every man, woman, and child of the human race, not just to us Jews."

Beginning with the *Pentateuch* and continuing through the Prophets and the *Psalms*, Thomas explained to Artie the truth of the Scriptures. He told how *Yahweh's* purpose always had been to reach out to man and provide a way whereby man could be forgiven of his sins and become part of *Yahweh's* family. He said that *Yeshua* took on the form of a man, was born as a human baby to a virgin, lived a sinless life, and died on a cross as a sacrifice for mankind's sins. As *Yahweh's* "Sacrificial Lamb," *Yeshua* once and forever paid the price of sin for anyone who would accept His precious gift. As *Yeshua* said on the cross, "*It is finished.*"[17] "Articus, that includes you. No other price is required; only your acceptance of the one *Yeshua* paid on His cross.

In conclusion, Thomas asked Articus the question all men must answer:

"What will you do with *Yeshua*? Will you trust Him to forgive you for your sins and become your Lord and your Savior, or will you reject His offer? If you were wounded in battle and lay dying in the arms of a fellow soldier, wouldn't you want to know that at death you would go directly to the arms of your loving Savior in heaven and be there forever? The choice is yours. No one else can make that decision for you."

Artie sat for a long time in deep contemplation. Was it possible to know your sins in this life would be forgiven and you would go to heaven when you died? How could that be? Would *Yahweh* admit a person into heaven simply because they placed their faith and trust in *Yeshua's* life and the blood He shed on that cross? Artie wanted to believe it was possible but needed to think through this most critical decision more clearly. That would take more time.

Finally, he spoke…

"I truly am grateful you have taken the time to tell me so much about *Yeshua* and of your faith in Him. As I understand it, you fully believe He is the answer to what life is all about. You have given me a lot to think about, and I suspect what you say may be the absolute truth. But this is a lot to comprehend, and I need time to think through all I have seen and heard these past few days before I can ever believe as do you. Because the matter is so critical, I promise I will give much thought to all I have heard while here in Jerusalem and will weigh your words carefully. However, I must return to my garrison in Caesarea and had meant already to be on my way. Even though the day is growing late, I hope to get on the road and make some progress before it gets too dark."

Though Thomas was disappointed the young man did not take the step of faith necessary to become *Yeshua's* follower, he could sense that the Holy Spirit already was at work in Artie's heart. Thomas knew that God's timing would be right in that decision. As he had since he first met Artie, Thomas committed in his heart to continue praying that what he had spoken to the young officer *"would not return void."*[18] He called for his sister to bring Artie's cloak and show the soldier out and back to the main street. As the two men parted ways, Thomas said, "I am asking *Yahweh's* protection as you travel home, and for His *Holy Spirit* to work in your mind and on your heart as you seek His truth. I also am praying that *Yeshua* will reveal Himself to you in your search." Thomas then returned to his work while Abigail helped Artie collect his things and prepare to leave.

Notes

1. The five books of Moses constituting the *Pentateuch* (first five books in the *Old Testament*)
2. Matthew 3:1–2
3. Matthew 3:3
4. John 1:29
5. Matthew 3:16–17
6. Genesis 49:8–12
7. Isaiah 53
8. Matthew 24:35
9. Isaiah 52:7
10. John 19:38–42
11. Luke 24:13-35
12. John 20:26

13. John 20:24–28
14. John 1:1–5
15. John 1:12
16. Ecclesiastes 7:20; Psalm 14:1; 53:1; 143:2
17. John 19:30
18. Isaiah 55:11

CHAPTER
2 8
ABIGAIL

"Like a lily among the thorns, so is my darling among the maidens."

Song of Solomon 2:2

Artie followed Abigail to the door and was about to speak when she spoke first. Thinking out loud she said: "If I recall you are assigned to Caesarea, and Jerusalem can be difficult to navigate if you are unfamiliar with our lanes and alleyways. Perhaps I should take you to the market street where you more easily can find your way."

Artie expressed appreciation for her offer to help, asking if it would meet the approval of Thomas. Her response was "Yes, as long as one of the household girls can go with us." At Abigail's call a young servant girl appeared, and together the three headed out the door. After only a short distance Artie realized he could find the way by himself but didn't want his time with Abigail to end too quickly. Even so, far too soon they came to a large cross-street that clearly led to the central market, and Abigail said, "I don't think you will have any trouble finding your way from here." Still fighting for time with her, Artie asked, "Could we find a place to sit down and talk for a few minutes?" Concerned about what people would think seeing a Jewish girl talking with a strapping young Roman soldier, Abigail looked around nervously and at the servant girl accompanying them and said, "Perhaps for just a moment."

Looking about, Artie saw a short stone wall encircling a stout olive tree about twenty feet tall with many gnarled and twisted limbs of various sizes and lengths. Olive trees grow slowly and widen in girth as they age, and Artie pegged this tree to be quite ancient, perhaps several hundred years old. However, its abundant crop of green, bright new olives, gave evidence it had been well cared for during all these years.

"Would over there in the shade of that olive tree be alright?" he asked.

Abigail nodded "yes" and motioned to the servant girl to wait for them on a bench under another nearby olive tree. As Abigail sat down where Artie had suggested, she made certain the "people distance" between them was sufficient not to evoke unwanted stares from passers-by. Not knowing what to say, she waited for the handsome young man near her side to speak.

Nervously he asked, "May I call you Abigail, and would you call me Artie?"

After a long pause she replied "Yes," and the ice was broken.

"Thank you," he said, "I really like hearing the sound of your voice." Then he asked, "Do you know why I came to see your brother?"

"Partially," she said. "I am afraid the curtains in our doorways do not make very good doors. They give a measure of privacy from sight, but not much from conversations unless they are whispered. I didn't mean to eavesdrop, but I heard you speaking with my brother about *Yeshua*, and I am curious as to why."

In response, Artie told her about having been sent by his centurion to Joppa to get Peter, his conversations with Peter, his astonishment at seeing Cornelius and his household become believers in *Yeshua*, and then learning that his own father apparently had become a believer. Artie told her he found it all so strange and rather unbelievable that he had embarked on a personal mission to find out the truth about this mysterious *Yeshua*. He then asked Abigail what she thought about it all.

She told him that after their parents died, she and Thomas went to live with their uncle. As a kind and loving big brother, Thomas did his best to look after her needs, but she often felt lonely and fearful, wondering about her life if something happened to him. Then Thomas was asked by *Yeshua* to travel with Him and learn about a new plan *Yahweh* had for all people, not just the Jewish nation. She was safe in her uncle's home and happy that Thomas had the wonderful opportunity to learn from such a knowledgeable teacher, but his absences only made her lonelier and more fearful.

Abigail continued, "During the three years Thomas spent with *Yeshua*, I always rejoiced when he came home for short periods of time and told of incredible experiences—seeing *Yeshua* heal sick people, calm stormy seas, teach better than the wisest priest or scribe ever had, and even raise a dead man back to life. At first, I wondered if my brother had been taken in by a mystic or charlatan. But that didn't make sense because Thomas always has been one who doubted everything and carefully investigated any new thing which came to his attention.

"Then when I finally met *Yeshua* in person I heard Him teach like no one I'd ever heard before. As I heard Him explain that the ancient list of laws and commandments given by our revered prophet of old, Moses, were to be replaced by a new system 'written on our hearts,'[1] something inside of me said, *I am hearing the truth; Yeshua must be the Son of Yahweh!* It was then I fell at His feet and received Him as my Savior and Redeemer! I don't know when I first discovered I had 'become a new person,'[2] but the next time Thomas left to travel with *Yeshua* I no longer felt afraid or lonely. For me, that was a huge change in my life.

"Another big change was that *Yeshua* took away much of my shyness and gave me a desire to tell everyone I meet about Him and His life-changing message. If *Yeshua* could give me 'the peace which surpasses all understanding,'[3] I knew He could give it to all who receive Him as I did. Artie, my prayer is that you will come to know the truth about Him as I have, and that you will find the contentment in your life that I have in mine."

Artie stared at the ground a few moments before he was able to respond. "I would like to know more about all you and Thomas have said, but I am torn with many questions about *Yeshua* becoming a man just so he could die for my sins and give eternal life to me and all mankind. Like I told your brother, I just need time to think about all this."

Speaking of time, the evening was growing late, and Abigail knew it was time for her and the servant girl to return home. Sensing that their time together was over, Artie asked: "Would you mind if I came to see you again at your home? Even though you are Jewish, and I am a Roman soldier, do you think your uncle and Thomas would permit it?" She replied:

"There is a world of difference between our cultures, languages, beliefs, and customs. Normally, it would be very difficult for any Jewish family to agree to such a meeting, but since you want to learn more about *Yeshua* and His life plan for all people, I believe they might approve of such a meeting."

"So, you'd be willing to see me again if they approve?" asked Artie.

"Yes," agreed Abigail, "but you would need to speak to Thomas and my uncle again to ask their permission."

To that Artie readily agreed, saying, "I must return to my duty station in Caesarea now, but I will come back to Jerusalem as soon as possible and then speak to them about our meeting again." Arising from his seat on the stone wall, Artie offered his hand to assist Abigail, allowing it to linger a few extra seconds and found she did nothing to resist that. As they parted, she said: "I will pray that the *Spirit* of *Yahweh* will protect you as you journey and give you wisdom as you seek to know more about *Yeshua*." Saying goodbye, Abigail motioned to the servant girl it was time to leave. After a short distance, Abigail turned to see if the young soldier had started on his journey. He had not but was watching her every move. She smiled and turned toward home.

Notes

1. 2 Corinthians 3:3
2. 2 Corinthians 5:17
3. Philippians 4:17

CHAPTER
29

THE ATTACK

"Cursed is he who attacks his neighbor in secret."
Deuteronomy 27:24

Artie watched Abigail and the servant girl until they were out of sight before he turned toward the legion barracks of the Roman command of Jerusalem. He knew the barracks were near one of the city gates that led to the road to Caesarea and thought he remembered its exact location. However, Jerusalem was not like Rome, with its wide streets and boulevards, spacious gardens, and ornate shops, but instead had many twisty lanes and alleyways which made it difficult for newcomers to easily find their way. In the part of Jerusalem where he found himself, the streets were narrow, full of potholes and trash, and littered with garbage left over from vendors who were gone for the day. No doubt they would return tomorrow to hawk their wares once again, but for now the deepening shadows of dusk were creeping in, turning the deserted streets into a dark and confusing maze. As a stranger to the area and a Roman soldier, seen by many as a representative of the despised Rome and her military force, he had a heightened sense of wariness and concern for his personal well-being. "If ever Abigail's prayers for my protection were needed, certainly now is the time!" he thought. A certain foreboding began to envelop him as he sought to remember his way back to the barracks. It didn't help that as he passed, he noticed several unwelcome stares from rough-looking individuals, some who seemed to be lingering in the shadows with sinister thoughts on their minds. Artie cheered himself at the thought he might be near the barracks and the safety of fellow soldiers, but he was beginning to have doubts as to whether he was on the correct route. If he had been traveling with a colleague, he would not have been worried, as two Roman soldiers would be formidable adversaries if challenged by untrained ruffians. If he could come upon a Roman patrol or even some landmark he recognized, he would feel a lot more at ease.

Up ahead, Artie saw three men huddled around a small fire, warming their hands and laughing—perhaps over a joke. They seemed harmless enough, but as Artie drew nearer, he saw one of the men stop laughing and stare at him like a hungry wolf about to pounce on its prey. Soon enough the other two followed his example, and Artie knew there probably would be trouble before he reached the warmth and security of the barracks. He tensed a bit and felt for his *pugio*,[1] making sure it was sheathed properly and ready for use as needed.

As the young soldier approached, one of the trio began to provoke him with comments about his youthfulness, his appearance of being lost and afraid of the dark, and other catcalls designed to provoke a fight. Sensing they could win any fight they started, they continued their remarks:

"Boy, what's that in your coin purse—good Jewish shekels or perhaps some denarii with that ugly picture of your Caesar? Let's see it!" Not one to back down, Artie gripped his dagger tighter and addressed the man with the big mouth.

"Careful friend, you'd better watch your words and actions. You tread on dangerous ground when you make light of Caesar or the Emperor's Defense Force. You might be able to defeat a single soldier like me, but you and your ilk would soon feel the combined weight of the Roman Legions if you bring down one of their own." The braggart hesitated for a moment, but, driven by his lust for money and his hatred for the occupying Roman force, he began to circle Artie like a boxer in a ring. For just a moment, Artie lost sight of the other two men, which was a major mistake. Suddenly he felt a sharp pain to his back and a simultaneous blow to his head. The two actions combined knocked Artie out cold, leaving him fair prey for whatever they wanted to do with him.

Notes

1. A small dagger of wood or bone covered with hammered metal, crafted and honed to a sharp point, used by Roman soldiers. It was about 8" long with a 4" handle, topped by a knob for better control. Worn as a sidearm always on the left side, it was from 2 ½ - 3" wide and exceedingly lethal.

CHAPTER
30
VISIONS IN THE NIGHT

"Disquieting thoughts from visions of the night, when deep sleep falls upon people."

Job 4:13

In a vision, a girl stood in front of him, lovely as ever with her beautiful smile and the scent of jasmine. Speaking to him in a quiet voice she told him that she loved him and would be by his side forever, no matter the differences in their lives due to religion, culture, race, or background. He tried to speak, but only drifted deeper into sleep with pain racking his head and body. Another vision came to him. In it his centurion, Cornelius, was speaking to him telling him that the Jewish carpenter was indeed the Son of *Yahweh* who loved him and died for his sins that he might spend eternity with those who called upon *Yeshua* for salvation.

How long these visions or dreams continued, Artie did not know. Finally, he dreamed he was traveling down a long tunnel that emerged into a small room where he found himself lying on a bed, not knowing where he was, how he got there, or in whose care he was. He tried to sit up, but the pain in his head and back was terrific, and he was forced to return to a prone position. His head hurt terribly, and he had to cover his eyes to shield them from light coming from a clay lamp near his bed.

    Slowly Artie turned first to his right and then to his left before he saw someone curled up asleep nearby, lying on a low couch of pillows with their head resting on their clasped hands, folded as if in prayer. As his eyes began to focus, he saw that it was Abigail. How could that be? He must surely be dreaming as he had left her just a short while ago to walk back toward the barracks in Jerusalem. Why was he in this room, and how did he get here? Slowly he remembered his encounter with the ruffians and their aggressive move to snatch his coin purse, but then what had happened? Then he remembered the sharp pain to his back and blow to his head. What happened next? All he knew was that his head hurt like crazy, and he felt nauseated when he tried to sit up. About that time his stirring about caused Abigail to awaken and jump up from her couch to see what he needed.

    "Lie still, Artie. You have a nasty head wound and have been unconscious for almost two days. When you were brought here you seemed near death, and we wondered if you were going to make it. Now lie quietly and try not to sit up so soon."

    "Where am I, and how did I get here?" Artie asked. Abigail said he was back at the house where she and Thomas lived with their uncle, and Artie had been brought there by Claudius, Romulus's servant. She told him Claudius had been concerned that Artie might not be able to find his way through the twisted streets back to the Roman barracks, and for his safety in that part of the city. Claudius knew there were troublemaking Jewish Zealots living in the area, and he felt that a young Roman soldier by himself might be in danger as darkness fell.

"Claudius told us that as he was returning to our house he saw you up ahead, making a wrong turn down a side street that led to a less than savory part of Jerusalem. He called to you, but you did not hear him. Though he hastened to catch up with you, by the time he did you already were under attack by three ruffians. However, he doesn't think they were Zealots for, if they had been, you probably would not have survived. Claudius believes they simply were attempting to rob you.

"Claudius said while one was gaining your attention the other two picked up stones and threw them at you, striking you in both your back and your head. When you fell you went down hard on the cobble stones. He yelled at the men who in the darkness may have thought he was a fellow soldier. At any rate, all three took off running before they even succeeded in robbing you. Claudius said you were lucky they didn't strip you naked, taking your clothes, dagger, coin purse and sandals, and leave you for dead. After considering where you were, Claudius realized our house was the nearest place of safety. With the help of a friendly passerby, he brought you here for us to care for you."

Hearing what happened and how fortunate he was to have survived the attack made Artie very thankful that Claudius had rescued him. When he asked about Claudius, Abigail said Thomas had a friend, a renowned physician currently in Jerusalem, and had asked Claudius to bring him to their home to treat Artie's wounds. That news made him even more appreciative of the risk Claudius had taken on his behalf. About then Artie's head began throbbing again. Reaching up to touch where he had been hit, he found the spot bandaged with a cloth of spun flax. Just the slightest pressure hurt so much that Artie cried out in pain. Then he fell back on his pillow and closed his eyes.

"Just rest," said Abigail, and she left the room as he fell back to sleep.

CHAPTER

31

THE PHYSICIAN

"Luke, the beloved physician, sends you his greetings."

Colossians 4:14

The man who entered the room clearly was not Jewish, or so it seemed to Artie. He was likely a middle-aged man with short salt-and-pepper hair and no beard. His clothes indicated Greek culture more than either Jewish or Roman. He had on a pleated Chiton,[1] which came to his knees, and a Chlamy,[2] which he wore as a cloak fastened at his waist by an ornamental clasp that depicted the head of an ox. He did not speak with a Hebrew accent, but clearly was comfortable with both Greek and Roman dialects.

"Well, my young friend, I see you have tired of sleeping and decided to favor us with your presence and speech once again. I am sure you probably are a bit perplexed as to your present circumstances and the prospects of your recovery. Do you know who you are and where you are at this moment?"

After recalling he was in the home of Thomas, Artie slowly pushed himself up against the wall where his makeshift bed was positioned. Then, with a sustained grimace he said: "I know who I am, but who are you? I don't think you are Jewish, and I suspect you are Greek by birth, am I right?"

Chuckling, the man replied: "You are totally right my young friend. My name is Luke,[3] and by trade I am a man of the healing arts. I studied medicine in my own country far away, and I journeyed to Jerusalem for a while to work here and visit many friends, including Thomas. After your unfortunate encounter with local thieves, he asked if I would come by and tend to your wounds. You are very fortunate that Claudius happened along at the right moment, or your outcome might have been very different. Now, let me examine the wound on your head."

Artie felt better just knowing he was in the presence of a trained doctor, and willingly allowed Dr. Luke to examine his head wound. Slowly unwinding the bandage as not to cause any more pain than necessary, the physician carefully examined the laceration while talking, mainly to himself.

"Doing well for such a short time since the incident. Ah, if only we oldsters healed as fast as the young, healthy ones do."

Turning to Abigail, Dr. Luke said: "I have prepared a poultice for his wound from the hyssop plant with its healing oils, as well as a few other herbs for pain relief. Periodically, I suggest you warm the mixture of wild ginger with wine I have prepared and give it to him to help prevent nausea. Also, you will need to change the covering on his wound every day until it heals; I have brought along a supply of soft coverings for that purpose." Turning back to Artie he said: "Over time, the pain will lessen, and you should heal completely and be none the worse for wear. Now let me see your back."

Painfully Artie leaned forward, allowing the doctor to examine a large bruise with an angry, greenish-blue color surrounded by red inflamed skin. Dr. Luke took a close look and felt the margins, causing Artie to clinch his teeth and grimace once more in pain. Satisfied with what he saw, the doctor stepped back and spoke to him: "You were a bit luckier there. You were somewhat protected from the blow by your cloak, so your skin was not broken.

"Now tell me, young man, why did a Soldier of Rome come to Jerusalem to learn more about *Yeshua?* I am overjoyed to know of your quest, but it is somewhat of a surprise to me!"

Artie settled back against the wall, once more resting against the cushion Abigail had placed there for his back and looked at the doctor quizzically and asked, "Did you know *Yeshua*? Did you actually speak to him or were you in his presence before he died?"

"No, I never met *Messiah*, but I have accepted Him as my Lord and Savior. May I tell you my story?"

"Please do," declared Artie, directing his full attention to the doctor. Abigail then excused herself to prepare some food and drink for her patient, asking Dr. Luke if he also would like to eat something. The doctor declined while also advising her not to give Artie too much food for a few days. After she left, the doctor made himself comfortable next to Artie's pallet, seating himself on the floor, which was cushioned by rugs stacked thickly for that purpose.

He began: "I come from a long line of physicians and was born and raised in Antioch, Syria. I always have been interested in the healing arts and knew at an early age I would become a physician. Thankfully, I was accepted at the finest medical school in all of Syria, the Hippocrates Medical School of Antioch, where my father also taught. I always have felt a passion to help alleviate suffering and pain in this world and have a strong belief that *Yahweh* has given us plants, herbs, and other of His creations to treat the illnesses and maladies one finds in this world. Because of that belief I have traveled to many places looking for and studying remedies used by the people there and have written a manual of medical practice to share with others what I have discovered.

"While treating patients in Antioch[4] I came across a man whose name had been changed from Saul to Paul. He was very passionate about his Jewish heritage and formal education in the best schools where he dutifully learned the laws of Judaism. He was especially proud of having been chosen to sit at the feet of a man named Gamaliel, one of the foremost teachers of the law. Though Gamaliel was a moderate Pharisee, Saul was a Zealot, and was incensed by the intrusion into Judaism of *Yeshua's* teaching which, some said, was 'turning the world upside down.'[5] Because of Saul's fierce defense of the Jewish Law, he was authorized by the Jewish leadership to track down Jews who had become followers of *Yeshua*, even bringing them back to Jerusalem for punishment. He was on his way to Damascus, Syria, for that purpose when he had a remarkable encounter with *Yeshua*, which left him blinded temporarily.[6] After that experience on the road to Damascus, Saul became as passionate—no, even more passionate—about following

Yeshua and His teachings than he had been about strict observance of the Jewish laws and commands.

"Saul's encounter left him with a variety of health issues, which prompted him to come to me for medical aid when he was in Antioch. (By the time we met, he had become known as Paul rather than Saul.) Paul's infectious passion for *Yeshua* eventually led me also to accept Him as my Savior, and Paul and I became lifelong friends. I even took leave of absence from my medical practice, often traveling with him as his personal physician. In the course of time, I sensed that *Yahweh* wanted me to write down the events which happened on our journeys. Thus, a permanent account could be recorded for use in telling many others about *Yeshua* and His teachings.[7] *Yahweh* wants the truth about His Son available throughout the ages to those of every race, culture, and background. That truth is the *Good News* that all can be set free from their sin and be reconciled to *Yahweh* by accepting the life, death, and resurrection of *Yeshua*."

Suddenly Artie interrupted Dr. Luke: "If I believed in gods, I might understand that one would come to earth in human form to see what we are doing. What I cannot understand is why one would come to earth in the likeness of a human being, knowing that he would die at the hands of those he came to help."

"Young soldier, if you will be patient with me, let me take you back to the beginning of time.

"*Yahweh* created the world as a place of perfection, including a beautiful garden where He placed the man and woman He made, Adam and Eve. They were to live in that garden, which was named Eden, joyfully and without any concerns, forever. Within it He made provision for all their needs. They had only one restriction: not to eat fruit from the Tree of the Knowledge of Good and Evil. *Yahweh* said to Adam and Eve: '*The day you eat of it you will surely die.*' But the leader of the nether world, the devil, tricked them, persuading them that *Yahweh* really didn't mean what He said, and so they ate from that tree.[8]

"As a Soldier of Rome, you understand what it means to be under authority, and that you must obey that authority.[9] You also know that when Rome or your centurion tells you, 'No,' you must obey, or there will be consequences. Without consequences, there is no law.

"*Yahweh* is the highest authority that exists. You may not realize it young man, but *Yahweh's* laws and commands are the basis of the Roman law you obey and defend.

For Rome to be just, it must mete out the punishment for various infractions set forth in the law. For *Yahweh* to be just, He had to take the action He said He would. So, Adam and Eve died, as have all their descendants down through the ages. By taking that action, *Yahweh* demonstrated that He means what He says, and that He requires obedience to His laws and decrees.

"However, *Yahweh* also is merciful, and He had a plan from the beginning of time as to how people could be brought back into favor with Him. That plan did not do away with His punishment for sin but provided a way of escape after their death to avoid eternity in hell, spending it instead with Him and *Yeshua* in heaven. That plan was for people to acknowledge and receive *Yeshua* as His son, repent (or turn from) their sins, and accept *Yeshua's* death and resurrection as payment for those sins. As *Yeshua* Himself has said: '*The one who hears My word and believes in Him who sent Me has eternal life and does not come into judgment. He has passed out of death into life.*'[10]

"Young man, I believe the real and only God of the Universe has put into the hearts of all people at our birth a deep desire for the answer to three questions: *Who am I? Where do I come from?* and *What happens to me at my death?* All people struggle to answer these questions during their lives. It is my sincere belief that only in *Yeshua* are the answers to each of these questions.

"In many ways, *Yahweh* is three entities in one. Over the course of history, He has revealed Himself as God the Father, God the Son, and God the Holy Spirit. In one respect we have within our own beings a parallel to His three entities: a distinct physical body, a distinct personality, and a distinct spark of life known as our soul. I believe this because mankind was created in *Yahweh's* own image[11] to have fellowship with Him.[12] In contrast, He created angels to be His ministering servants.[13] For a time *Yeshua* and mankind were made lower than the angels, but through *Yeshua's* death on the cross, *Yeshua* was sanctified and raised higher than the angels. This made it possible for men to be brought to glory and given the title of 'brothers and sisters' by *Yeshua*.[14]

"To enjoy complete fellowship with another person requires a sort of 'give-and-take,' an ability to reason and choose whether to agree or disagree. As *Yahweh's* ministering servants, angels lack that ability. But for we humans to be considered 'brothers and sisters of *Yeshua*,' *Yahweh* wanted us to have that ability.

"The ability to reason and think for oneself is what happened in the Garden of Eden. *Yahweh* told Adam and Eve what would happen if they ate from the Tree of the Knowledge of Good and Evil. Satan disputed that statement, and the pair were free to choose whom to believe, *Yahweh* or Satan. That 'freedom of choice' has continued down through the ages. Through repentance and obedience to Him, we can choose to love *Yahweh* as He loves us, or we can reject Him in favor of Satan's lie. *Yahweh* wants that choice to be through the free will He has given us; not something that causes us to respond mechanically, as though we are His servants and not His children."

After sitting still for so long while Dr. Luke spoke, Artie shifted position, which made him grimace in pain. Then he asked, "If *Yahweh* is so all-powerful, why wouldn't all mankind want to obey Him to avoid suffering the consequences of disobedience?" Dr. Luke responded by explaining the nature of Satan and the temporary hold he has been given over the world.

"Because *Yahweh* is Holy, His very nature is the opposite of unholy, and He cannot entertain the concept of sin or unholiness in His presence. Among His created angels was one who reveled in his own beauty and wisdom. Those attributes caused that angel to sin and commit violence, so *Yahweh* cast out of His presence him and fellow angels who joined in his rebellion.[15] Ever since, that angel—known as the devil or Satan—has sought to drive a wedge between

Yahweh and His creation, beginning in the Garden of Eden with the first man and woman.

"In the years since then, the Devil has strongly influenced man to believe he can be his own god and master of his own soul. By the independent nature *Yahweh* has given us, people everywhere seek their own desires and find it easy to succumb to the devil's urgings. This leads us into the same path of sinful rebellion that caused Satan himself to lose fellowship with *Yahweh* in heaven. But since *Yahweh* created us to have fellowship with Him both now and for eternity, He wanted to provide a way for people to overcome that sin and be reconciled to Him. He accomplished this through the virgin birth, sinless life, cruel crucifixion, and glorious resurrection of His only Son, *Yeshua*. By allowing His blood to be shed on the cross, *Yeshua* opened the door for anyone who would accept that sacrifice to become a child of *Yahweh*.

"Artie, like every other man or woman on earth, you have the freedom to accept or reject *Yeshua's* sacrifice for your sins. I choose *Yeshua*. How will you choose?"

"Doctor, what you say is both informative and very troubling. In my brief stay here in Jerusalem I have learned a great deal about *Yeshua* and his life, but I need more time to think it all through and give it proper consideration."

"My young friend, do not wait too long. You learned how near death can be when you were set upon by those ruffians. Who knows, but that *Yahweh* sent along Claudius to give you an extra opportunity to accept his love and gift of eternal life? As a soldier of Rome, any assignment can put you in harm's way. There's a saying that 'cats have nine lives.' To the best of my knowledge, that isn't said of men, especially soldiers!"

With that Dr. Luke rose to leave his patient. "I need to check on my other patients now, but I will keep you in my prayers. Follow my instructions for the next few weeks, and you soon should be back to your normal health. Even more important, consider carefully what you have learned during your visits with me and others here in Jerusalem, and don't delay too long in making your choice!"

Notes

1. A type of tunic that fastens at the shoulders or waist, usually gathered in folds from the waist to the knee.
2. A top cloak made of heavier material and used as a coat.
3. Colossians 4:14
4. Acts 11:26: Believers were first called Christians in Antioch. Before that they were known as "Followers of *Yeshua*" or "Followers in the Way."
5. Acts 17:6
6. Acts 22:3–16
7. Luke wrote "The Gospel of Luke" and "The Book of Acts."
8. Genesis chapter three
9. Matthew 8:9
10. John 5:24
11. Genesis 1:27
12. 1 Corinthians 1:9
13. Hebrews 1:14
14. Hebrews 2:9–12
15. Ezekiel 28:12–19

CHAPTER
32
THE LEAVE-TAKING

"Let me see your face; let me hear your voice. For your voice is pleasant, and your face is lovely."

Song of Solomon 2:14b

Just as Dr. Luke was leaving the room, Abigail returned.

"Leaving, Doctor?" she asked.

"Yes. Artie is mending nicely but won't be ready to return to active duty for a few weeks. As for returning to Caesarea, that will be whenever he feels up to the journey. In the meantime, I leave him in your care." As he reached for his cloak and walking stick, Luke turned to Artie with these parting words: "I am praying for you, young man. I believe our Lord has great plans for you that you don't want to miss."

After Luke left, Artie asked Abigail to bring his uniform so he could dress. To her question of "Why?" he replied: "I already have overstayed the time off I requested from my centurion, and I need to return before he thinks I have become a deserter."

Over her objections—and though he clearly needed more time to recuperate—Artie made it quite clear he was determined to dress and leave that very day, so with reluctance she brought his things. As he dressed, she left the room, returning when he called her name. Seeing him once again resplendent in his military uniform, Abigail's emotions went from being his nurse to those of a young woman wondering what it would be like to be held in his strong young arms.

With all the courage a nervous young man in love could muster—and hampered by the fact that neither *Hebrew* nor *Aramaic* were his native tongues—Artie launched into his farewell speech.

"I am very sorry for all the trouble I've caused you, Thomas, and your family, and I'm deeply thankful for the care and hospitality everyone has shown me. Never in my life has anyone demonstrated the care and personal attention you have given me! Also, please tell Claudius how grateful I am to him for saving my life and bringing me here!

"Even before you became my nurse you have been in my thoughts. From that first time we met in the Caesarea market I have not been able to stop thinking of you. I know we come from two very different worlds and how much animosity the Jewish people have toward us Romans, but I want very much to see you again. Is there any way your family might give permission for that to happen, or is that asking for the impossible?"

"Artie, I also would like very much to see you again, as I told you earlier. My brother and Dr. Luke have seen how polite and courteous you are, and I think they can tell that I have become quite fond of you. So, when I ask permission for us to visit each other, I feel certain they will say, 'Yes.' As you know, we bring our candles to sell in the Caesarea market regularly, and I could send you a message telling you when that would be."

Artie continued his farewell remarks: "I realize how much you and your family are hopeful about my acceptance of *Yahweh* as the one true god and *Yeshua* as his son. I have learned so much about them these past few days and have been the personal recipient of the love and care for others that come from those who trust in him. As a Roman soldier, I am trained to carefully consider the facts and situation, even in the heat of battle, reasoning them out to reach the best decision possible. At this point, I still am confused by many things and need time to sort them out in my mind."

As they said their goodbyes, each instinctively held out their hands to one another, so their fingers briefly touched. Taking advantage of the moment, Abigail pulled a small parchment scroll tied with a blue ribbon from her pocket and slipped it into Artie's hand, saying he was not to open it until the *Spirit of Yahweh* let him know the time had come. Then she called for a male servant to take Artie back to the Jerusalem gate that led to the road to Caesarea, and they parted.

As he was about to go through the gate, he glanced up at its impressive architecture and noticed a small yellow bird perched on its pinnacle appearing to look directly at him! "Little friend," he thought, "are you part of a flock, or have you been assigned to watch over me these past several weeks? Whichever the case, I always feel good when I hear your cheerful little song; just wish I knew what you were saying!"

CHAPTER
33

THE ROAD TO CAESAREA

"You can enter God's Kingdom only through the narrow gate. The highway to hell is broad, and its gate is wide for the many who choose that way. But the gateway to life is very narrow and the road is difficult, and only a few ever find it."

Matthew 7:13–14 (NLT)

Leaving Jerusalem for Caesarea, Artie had to choose between two routes. The better-known would take him through the pass of Beth-horon, but that was several miles longer than the road through Antipatris.[1] Even so, reaching that town still meant a trek of some forty-two miles. However, when he arrived in Antipatras, Artie would be only twenty-six miles from Caesarea.

As a Roman soldier, Artie was trained to march twenty-five miles a day with a light kit and twenty with a full field pack. Normally the trip from Jerusalem to Caesarea would take about three days. But with his bandaged wounds and weakened condition, Artie knew it would take longer. "However," he thought, "I still might make it in three more days if I walk a few miles this afternoon before it gets too dark."

His visit to Jerusalem had been intense. First came his appointment with the centurion, Romulus, then the unexpected visit to the home of Thomas, *Yeshua's* friend and disciple, followed by the attempt on his life by murderous thieves, and his miraculous rescue by Romulus's servant, Claudius. Then, badly injured, he had been taken back to Thomas' home where he was attended to by Dr. Luke and cared for several days by Thomas' sister, Abigail. If that weren't enough, Abigail had stolen his heart and indicated she also had feelings for him and would ask for permission to see him next time she went to Caesarea to sell their candles! All of this would give him much to think about on the journey back to his post. And knowing that Abigail had feelings for him would make the trip easier despite the lingering pain from his wounds.

Having left Jerusalem late in the day, Artie would be walking well past the normal time when people obtained lodging for the night. Not wanting to lose time seeking it out, Artie decided he simply would find a safe place off the main road where he could camp for the night. Besides, he wanted to be alone with his thoughts.

Spotting a small grove of olive trees about a hundred yards to his left, he wasted no time in checking it out. He found that others had camped there in the past and had built a firepit and cleared underbrush to make a proper campsite. In addition, a small well was located at the northern edge of the stand of trees. With these discoveries he laid down his pack, gathered twigs and small limbs to make a fire, and selected leafy branches and grass as padding for his sleeping mat. That done, he spread his extra travel cloak to lay down on, planning to use his uniform *Chlamy* as his covering for the night.

With his housekeeping chores completed, Artie retrieved from his backpack a small portion of fish and bread he had purchased at a roadside stand as he left Jerusalem. Quickly consuming his meal, he washed it down with the remaining water in his travel pouch. Made of goatskin sewed tightly together with animal hair, when empty and filled with one's breath it could make a reasonably comfortable pillow. While at the well, Artie drew a bucket of fresh water to wash away the grime and dirt of the day from his arms, legs, and feet. He concluded his wash-up by pulling off his shirt, leaning over and emptying the bucket over his head to wash his hair, face, and wounds on his torso. His ablutions completed, he dried himself off, rebandaged his wounds as best he could, and pulled his shirt back on, remembering fondly the gentle touch of Abigail when she had cleansed and bandaged them. "Ah, if only she could be here now!" Then he was ready for bed.

With the last rays of light playing out against the sky, Artie settled his lanky frame comfortably on his mat. While it lacked the comfort of his pallet back at base or the bed Abigail had made for him at Thomas' house, it was sufficient for him to elicit a mighty yawn as he stretched his body from head to toes and settled down to sleep. With the blackness of night closing in around him and stars illuminating the vast heavens, twinkling like a sea of diamonds, he knew sleep wouldn't be long in coming.

Despite his weariness from the day's activities and continuing pain from his wounds, Artie couldn't help but think about what he saw in the sky above. He recalled something his centurion had said when speaking about *Yahweh*:

The heavens declare the glory of Yahweh, and the skies proclaim the work of His hands. Day after day they pour forth speech; night after night they reveal knowledge. They have no speech, they use no words; no sound is heard from them. Yet their voice goes out into all the earth, their words to the ends of the world.[2]

For the first time, the full impact of that statement was very real to Artie. *Does not what I am seeing testify to intelligent order and design?* he thought. *Just look at the majesty of the heavens, which seem to have no beginning or end. The stars, the moon, the sun all follow a prescribed order. They don't speak and have no words, but their orderliness in repeating their rounds every day and night throughout the ages speaks volumes. It couldn't have "just happened" without a plan and someone to make it happen!*

All his life Artie had heard of many so-called "gods," beings like *Primordial,* a group of gods which came before all others, *Ciros,* god of heavenly constellations and the measure of the year, *Helios,* the sun god, *Zeus,* known as "the father of gods and men," and *Chaos,* a god who filled the gap between heaven and earth and created the first beings. *Chaos!* he thought. *Certainly that could not be one who brings order and sense to the universe like what I'm seeing in the heavens this night!* Most of all, he had been taught that Caesar himself was a god and worthy of worship. In fact, as a soldier he had sworn an oath to honor Rome and Caesar above all else.

Artie often had wondered how everything came into being. Though Caesar claimed to be a god, Artie realized the Roman emperor was just a human being with all the faults and failures of other human beings. As Artie reflected on what he had learned about *Yeshua* from those in Jerusalem who knew him as well as from Cornelius, he realized that *Yahweh* and *Yeshua* were very different from all those other so-called "gods." It seemed to him that those "gods" were only figments in the imaginations of people who felt some how they offered good luck, power, or success to their followers. Yet he had seen no proof that such results ever occurred…nothing that even remotely matched the evidence he had seen and experienced from the disciples of *Yeshua*. His miracles, the prophetic writings of ancient sages which had been fulfilled in *Yeshua's* life, death, and resurrection, and the strength of conviction among those committed to continue his ministry did not point either to a mad man or an imaginary being. Rather, they gave evidence of a supernatural being who loved humanity enough to give himself as sacrificial payment for the wicked and deceitful hearts[3] and lives all men possess. Artie knew he did not understand all he had seen and heard, but he did know he was much closer to the truth about the purpose of life, self-worth and dignity, love and serving others than he'd ever been before.

Looking up into the night sky, he spoke what was on his heart: "I am still reasoning things out in my mind, and I look forward to talking them over with my centurion. But I do know how what I have heard and seen has opened my eyes and caused my heart to burn within me.[4] I ask that You protect me on my trip home and harmonize my heart and mind to clearly understand the decision I must make."

Artie calmed his thoughts. Even though his decision was yet to be made, somehow, he knew *Yahweh* would help him work things out. Then, feeling a peace that surpassed all his understanding,[5] he drifted softly to sleep under the calm night sky, not realizing that the small yellow bird was resting high above his head in an ancient olive tree.

Notes

1. This was the route taken by the Roman soldiers in Acts 23:31 when the apostle Paul was taken from Jerusalem to Caesarea.
2. Psalm 19:1–4
3. Jeremiah 17:9
4. Luke 24:31–32
5. Philippians 4:7

CHAPTER
34
THE JOURNEY HOME

"If God be with me and keep me safe on this journey that I take...then the Lord will be my God."

Genesis 28:20–21

A small shaft of sunlight shot between the branches and leaves of the old olive trees scoring a direct hit on the eyelids of the fitfully sleeping young Artie. A frown crossed his face as his eyes reacted to the intense rays of morning's first sunlight. Squinting as he raised his hand to block the offending intrusion, he struggled to gain consciousness as to where he was and why. About then, the wounds on his body and head reminded him of what he had been through, and he realized that a night of sleeping on the ground with little more padding than a mat and some underbrush had not been a good idea.

Why, oh why, didn't I listen to Abigail and stay there a few more nights while I healed?

That thought also renewed his feelings for her and how he ached to hear her voice and feel the touch of her hands. The best thing that had come from his run-in with the ruffians who injured him so badly was meeting her again and discovering what a difference she would make in his life.

He knew he should have listened to her pleas to wait a few days before returning to Caesarea, but he was worried that Cornelius might think of him as a deserter. As a soldier of Rome and because of his deep respect for his centurion, he did not want that to happen. He also realized how much Cornelius trusted in him, and he did not want to offend or disappoint him in that trust.

In-spite-of his pain and aches, Artie slowly rose to his feet. He would have considered spending another day camping there and nursing his painful wounds, but he wanted to be on his way as soon as possible. With a certain amount of grimacing and soft groans he lightly touched the bruised places on his torso, gently massaging them with some of the healing ointment Dr. Luke had given him. Fortunately, it was a beautiful morning with the promise of a cooler day ahead, which would make the journey a little easier. Several birds in the olive grove were calling back and forth to each other, telling the world what a beautiful day it was going to be. Their singing lifted the young soldier's mood, and he reasoned that "one of Caesar's finest" was tough enough to bear a bit of pain. Thus determined, he resolved to push on to reach Caesarea and his centurion in only two days if possible. Hastening to straighten out his uniform as much as possible and lacing his sandals tightly, he cleaned up his campsite, gathered up his meager belongings and headed for the highway. There would be much to share with Cornelius on his return to Caesarea.

Though the day was early, already there were travelers moving along the road toward Antipatris. In addition to herdsmen driving their flocks of goats along the highway, here and there he spotted lone individuals or small groups of travelers hurrying along and carrying personal belongings or wares of assorted things. A few camels plodded listlessly, chewing their cud blissfully as their masters tried to prod them on, barking orders that were for the most part ignored. Artie fell in among the crowd, determined to make it to Antipatris by nightfall.

Rounding a sharp bend around a hillside, Artie caught sight of two fellow officers about fifty yards ahead. As he drew near, he could tell from their laughter and the way they seemed to be lurching about and leaning on each other's shoulders that they hadn't yet shaken off the effects of their prior night on the town, and still were trying to get their bearings. Drawing alongside, Artie greeted them and asked if he might join them on the trail. After returning his greeting they gave assent to his companionship commenting, "There's strength and safety in numbers." Artie told them his name and rank, stating that he was attached to the garrison in Caesarea under the command of Centurion Cornelius, "A good man and superior leader whom I respect greatly."

One of the two ventured that his name was Fortus, and his fellow soldier was Flavian.

"Flavian's name means 'yellow hair,'" Fortus added. "I guess they named him that because his hair is blond and curly. Lucky guy, the girls like to run their fingers through it." Flavian took a mock swing at his friend's arm as if to say, "Cool it." However, he seemed to like the remark about the girls. Fortus continued: "We are to report for duty in the city of Tyre a week from now but intend to spend every day until then checking out young ladies everywhere we stop for the night. We have a farther journey than you but will appreciate the added security of a fellow soldier as far as you go."

Noticing the bump on Artie's head and how he seemed to favor the side where he had been bruised, Fortus asked Artie to explain. Artie explained what had happened when he was set upon by three thugs in Jerusalem, saying that "If it had not been for the timely assistance of a friend, I most likely would have been killed." After a little more description of what had happened, Fortus and Flavian brought up stories of their own close calls, probably embellishing them a little for added attention.

As that conversation began to wear itself out, Artie turned to what was foremost on his mind:

"When I was being attacked so brutally in Jerusalem, I really thought for a moment my time was up. Knowing how hungry those thugs were for everything I had—my money, clothes, equipment—I greatly feared they would strip me and leave my naked body right there on that dark street in a town where no one knew me. My command in Caesarea would wonder what became of me, and I'd forever be known as a deserter and a renegade. Even worse than that, I wondered if the few years I've lived on this earth was all there was, or if there was an afterlife where my soul or spirit would go. What about you? In some of the scrapes you've had, did you ever have such thoughts?"

Artie's new travel companions looked at him as if to say, *What's wrong with this young soldier? Was he so traumatized by his near-death experience that he can't snap out of it? Will he be able to function fearlessly as a soldier of Rome?*

After a long pause, Flavian spoke: "I don't give a moment's thought to that ever happening. When your time comes, you're dead, and that's the end of it. On about every street corner you can find someone with a new god they claim rules in their life and who will protect them from harm. Yet these people die every day in all manner of deaths. I've seen life, and I've seen death. I'm going to live my life to the fullest and enjoy every moment of it. The way I see it, this life is all you have, and while I'm here I'm going to eat to my heart's content, drink joyfully, and use my body to make the ladies happy." Then Fortus spoke.

"My companion is still young and not yet tasted of the trials and tribulations of life as I have. Furthermore, he speaks without much knowledge of the wonders of creation around us or the real meaning of life." Gesturing with a wide sweep of his arms he asked: "Is all this around us a random act of a god or gods who are just toying with mankind and who care nothing about us as individuals? I don't know what to think about it all. I grew up in a home where we honored many Roman gods with prayers, offerings, and attempts at appeasement. But I never saw evidence that any of those so-called "gods" answered the prayers of me or my family or revealed themselves to us in any tangible way. When I left my father's house, I gave up on those 'higher powers' and, frankly, have given little thought to them since. As long as there are battles to fight for Rome and, as Flavian said, 'good food, strong drink, and beautiful women to comfort me when the battles are won,' then I am content."

Artie waited until both men had finished speaking.

"Have neither of you ever lain upon your sleeping mat late on a sleepless night and pondered such questions as *Where did I come from? Why am I here?* and *Where am I going when I die?* Are not these the thoughts and questions all men have?" After a long silence while each waited for the other to speak, they both nodded their heads indicating they had. After that acknowledgement, Artie continued.

"Fellows, a few weeks ago my centurion sent me to Joppa to escort an itinerant fisherman back to Caesarea so the man could speak to him. The fisherman was a disciple of a Galilean named *Yeshua*, who Rome crucified as an insurrectionist. As I talked with him on the return journey to Caesarea, I couldn't believe one as unlearned as he could speak so knowledgeably. Then, when we arrived in Caesarea and he addressed my centurion and his household, he said that the man Rome had crucified had been raised from the dead, that *Yeshua* was the son of an almighty god named *Yahweh*, and that he is now alive in heaven. While those who heard the fisherman speak were mesmerized, I was puzzled. Later, when I had the opportunity to speak privately to my centurion, I discovered that he too had begun to believe there was only one true god in heaven, which is why he had sent for the fisherman. Seeing how perplexed I was over the entire situation, he gave me leave time to go to Jerusalem to meet with those who had personal experience with *Yeshua*. While there, I met with the centurion who oversaw *Yeshua's* crucifixion, who had certified that he was dead, as well as with others who insisted strongly that he is alive. All of this has caused me to rack my brain and try to sort out truth from fiction. How can a man have been killed and yet still be alive? If such a man exists, could he actually be the son of the only true god? If there is such a god, does he know who I am? If he does, what difference does that make to him? Is it possible that such a god could personally care for me and be involved in my life? If so, why? How would that affect my life on earth? *Yeshua's* friends all say there is a real heaven and a hell, and that when we die our spirits live on forever, either in heaven or in hell. They would even say that my being here now and talking with the two of you is part of god's plan for all three of our lives."

As Artie shared all the happenings in his life since taking that strange trip to Joppa, he was surprised to find how happy he felt simply recounting those events, and how much he enjoyed telling the other two soldiers what he had learned about *Yeshua* and *Yahweh*. When he finished speaking, they were silent for a long time. Their discussions had made the day pass quickly, and lengthening shadows warned that dusk soon would be upon them. Up ahead to their right the men could see the outskirts of a village where there would be an inn with a room to be had, a hot meal to eat, and plenty of company for rounds of drinks and games of chance, and ladies seeking their companionship. As their thoughts turned to those pleasures, Fortus spoke.

"Enough of this depressing talk. I, too, have heard of this *Yahweh,* and I don't like what I've heard. Some say he will want me to give up wine, women, and song, and judge me harshly if I don't. I prefer what one of the most famous Jewish leaders, King Solomon, said about life, that man has no better thing to do under the sun except to eat, drink, and be merry[1], and I'm certainly ready for that. What about you Flavian?"

With a grin and quickening of his step, the younger man indicated he was ready for a hearty meal and a good time. Though they encouraged Artie to lighten up and join them in their festivities, he declined. He hoped to make it to Antipatris before his energy gave out, take a room there for the night, and then reach Caesarea before the next nightfall.

These were Artie's final words as they parted: "I hope I have not overburdened you with our conversation. I do not have words enough to express the deep longing in my heart to know the truth as to what life really is about, whether there is such a god as *Yahweh*, and if there is a purpose for my life here on earth other than just to live and move and have my being.[2] Each of us has to seek our own answers to whether there is deeper meaning to life than just our existence. As for me, though I still am searching for these answers, even the thought of this man *Yeshua* causes my heart to leap within me as being someone who is not just an ordinary man. My prayer for both of you is safety as you travel on to your destination, and like me, you will ask yourselves the questions I have presented and seek for the true meaning of life."

With a short round of farewells, the two men departed Artie's company and turned right toward the village while Artie turned left toward Antipatris. There he hoped to find a quiet inn where he could rest and tend to his wounds before pressing on the next day for the 26-mile walk from there to

Caesarea. Reflecting on the day he concluded that despite his pain, it had been good to share with others his quest for the truth. Though he was disappointed in their lack of more serious response to his conversation, just being able to talk with fellow Roman soldiers helped him shape his thoughts and sharpen the questions he would ask Cornelius.

After reaching Antipatris and his room for the night, Artie again played over in his mind what Dr. Luke and Thomas had told him. Both had spoken of something called the *Spirit of Yahweh* who drew men toward the truth. They said that without the *Spirit's* drawing, one could never know the safety and comfort of *Yahweh*. Was that why *Yeshua* came to earth? Was that *Spirit* drawing him to *Yahweh*? Though such thoughts might have troubled him a few weeks ago, now they gave him a strange sense of peace and comfort as he drifted off to sleep.

Notes

1. Ecclesiastes 8:15
2. Acts 17:28

CHAPTER
35

THE YELLOWHAMMER'S SONG

"...How can I describe the kingdom of God? What story should I use to illustrate it? It is like a mustard seed planted in the ground. It is the smallest of all seeds, but it becomes the largest of all garden plants; it grows long branches, and birds can make nests in its shade."

Mark 4:30–32

As he had hoped, three long days after leaving Jerusalem Artie limped up to the front gate of the Caesarea Roman garrison well into the second watch[1] of the night. The guard on duty called out, "Halt! Who goes there?" Even though the guard was from Artie's own unit, both Artie and his army uniform were in such sad shape he was barely recognizable.

"What happened to you, Sir? Are you alright; do you need help getting to your barracks?" After providing a brief explanation and assurance he could continue on his own, Artie stumbled to his barracks and his own sleeping space. Removing only his boots he crawled into bed, grateful to be home.

Though normally a morning person, it was nearly noon before Artie was awake and bathed, with his wounds bandaged and dressed. On his way to the mess hall, he went by the centurion's office to ask his chief of staff for an appointment "at the earliest opportunity." While eating he received a message from the chief that the centurion was expecting him at the beginning of the fourth watch.[2] With an appointment set, Artie returned to his quarters to review the events of his time in Jerusalem and to make certain he was looking his best when he met with Cornelius.

He thought back to when the centurion first had summoned him to his office in the Citadel, sharing his private thoughts with Artie on life and questioning whether it had meaning and purpose. Artie recalled how his superior officer had puzzled over the reality of gods and the shocking statement he had made: "I have felt strongly there really is but one Supreme Being, and that He is the only God who exists." That meeting began the strange odyssey on which Artie had been embarked ever since: first to Joppa to bring Peter, an itinerant fisherman, back to Caesarea to speak to the centurion about a man named *Yeshua*. Peter had traveled with *Yeshua*, who had been crucified in Jerusalem by Rome, but Peter said *Yeshua* had been raised back to life on the third day. The result of Peter's message was that Cornelius and his household believed Peter when he said that *Yahweh* was the one true God, and that humans could be adopted into his family.[3] Thereupon they received *Yeshua* as *Yahweh's Son* and their Savior.

Because of Artie's confusion over that turn of events, Cornelius sent him to Jerusalem to meet with the centurion who had overseen *Yeshua's* crucifixion, but that meeting yielded little of the information Artie was seeking. But as often happens in life situations, *Yahweh* opened doors for Artie to meet with men who had walked with *Yeshua* and with others whose first-hand knowledge corroborated Peter's story. *What a story I have to tell,* thought Artie, *but I wonder how my centurion will react when I tell him I still am weighing all I have seen, heard, and experienced concerning Yeshua and Yahweh.*

As on Artie's previous visits to his spacious office, Cornelius welcomed him more like a father than a commanding officer. But Artie sensed a major change in the centurion's demeanor since the last time he was there. Instead of worry, he saw contentment. And the warmth exuding from Cornelius's smile and the tone of his voice were those of a completely changed man. "Come in, Artie, and sit down. I really want to hear all about your experiences in Jerusalem!" While the office still held all the trappings of the garrison's senior officer, those things seemed to take second place to the scent of flowers and songs of birds coming from the atrium.

While Artie took his seat, Cornelius continued talking.

"I truly hated hearing about the injuries you suffered in Jerusalem from the thugs who set upon you. You were fortunate to have been rescued by Romulus's servant. Not only did he save your life, but he also reported what happened to Romulus, who sent me a post as to why you would be detained in returning. Without that knowledge, I would have had to report you AWOL.[4] From the moment I heard what had happened I began to pray to *Yahweh* for your recovery, and I am relieved to see how He has answered my prayers. You will need to be on light duty for a while, but I can see it will not be long before you're back in fighting form. Now tell me about everyone you saw in Jerusalem and what you have learned."

With that invitation, Artie told the centurion about those with whom he had met, including what they had to say about *Yeshua*.

"Everyone spoke very convincingly about his teachings and statement that he was the son of *Yahweh*. Some claimed to have seen him alive after his crucifixion, while others only had second-hand knowledge. The one who confused me most was Romulus, perhaps because he himself was confused. He said he had been there when a spear was thrust into *Yeshua's* side and had signed the death certificate. But the soldiers he posted at the tomb said they saw an angel roll the stone away from its opening,[5] the body was gone, and they fled in fright. Romulus said the men he hand-picked for that duty were among his finest, and not given to fear or flights of fancy. But their actions, including reporting to the chief priests what had happened instead of to him as their superior officer had left him wondering whom or what to believe. In-spite-of the passion with which others spoke about *Yeshua*, his confusion also has left me with a degree of doubt."

With Artie's words hanging in the air, both he and Cornelius sat quietly for a moment with the only sound being that of bird songs coming from the atrium.

"Articus, do you hear one bird singing above all the rest?"

Artie nodded "Yes."

"In my years here in Caesarea I have become fascinated with the great variety of birds. My favorite is that one, the Yellowhammer (*Emberiza Citrinella*)—not just because of the distinctive yellow spots on its black feathers—but because its high-pitched song sounds something like 'a little bit of bread and no cheese.' Articus, if you were to go into the atrium and look into the mustard bush, you could see it and be able to verify that what I am telling you is true. Do you want to go look?"

"No, I believe what you have said."

Cornelius continued. "When you have heard that particular warble before now, did you know it was a Yellowhammer?"

"No, but for many weeks, one often has seemed to be close by, and its song has both tantalized and haunted me. I, too, have thought its warble sounded like words, but just couldn't figure out what."

"Though neither of us can see it, you are willing to take my word that it is a Yellowhammer, is that right?"

"Yes."

"I know it's a Yellowhammer because of its distinctive voice, and you believe it is because you trust me to tell you the truth. In that same sense of reasoning, can you take a same step of faith when I tell you there is only one true God, *Yahweh*, and His only begotten Son is *Yeshua*?"

After thinking thoughtfully for a long time, Artie said, "I want to believe, but I need help with my unbelief."[6]

Speaking again, Cornelius said: "Articus, in Jerusalem you met with Romulus, a man you said was filled with confusion. You also met with several who believed in *Yeshua,* and from the sounds of what you have told me, there was no confusion among them. Is that right?"

"Yes."

"Well, one of the truths I have learned from Peter and other believers is that *Yahweh* is '*not a God of confusion, but a God of peace.*'[7] Another truth is this quote from one of the old

Hebrew scrolls concerning what *Yahweh* does when a person chooses to follow Him: '*I will give you a new heart and put a new spirit within you; and I will remove the heart of stone from your flesh and give you a heart of flesh. And I will put My Spirit within you.*'[8] Articus, you have known me ever since I brought you to Caesarea. Would you say I am the same centurion now after receiving *Yeshua* as my Savior and Redeemer that I was before my encounter with Peter?"

"No."

"Articus, from your time with me this afternoon, can you tell me in what way I may have changed?"

"Sir, you always have been very kind and thoughtful toward me, but today you do seem different, more like a caring friend than just my superior officer…and your eyes and face are almost as though you were a new man inside."

"Articus, I have had nothing to do with these changes. Even my servants have said it is easier to serve me than before, though I was never hard or cruel to them. But now I have been given that new *Spirit* promised in that Hebrew scroll. How did this change come about? It's through faith. You said Dr. Luke spoke to you about the apostle Paul. In one of his letters, Paul wrote that '*Faith is the substance of things hoped for, the evidence of things unseen.*' He went on to say that '*By faith we understand that the world has been created by the word of Yahweh so that what is seen has not been made out of things that are visible.*'[9] Articus, everywhere we look we see things man did not create—trees, flowers, birds, animals, rocks, rivers, and more. In some fashion they came into being. We can pretend they just happened to be what they are, or we come to believe that an

Intelligent Being created them. The oldest of the Jewish scrolls identifies that 'Being' as I AM, or *Yahweh*. As I listened to Peter, studied with him while he was here, and have continued to study with my Hebrew servants, there is no doubt in my mind that *Yahweh* is the great I AM who created the world and everything in it, including mankind, and that *Yeshua* is His one and only Son. Through faith in Him and Him alone, *Yahweh* adopts us into His family to be His sons and daughters and to be brothers and sisters with *Yeshua*.[10]

"It has been said that faith means something when you do not understand the 'Whys.' *Yahweh* never condemns us for asking 'Why?' In the ultimate analysis, the question is not 'Why?' but 'Who?' *Yahweh* calls on us to believe *Yeshua*, who said: '*I am the Way, the Truth, and the Life. No man comes to Yahweh but by Me. I am the resurrection and the life. He who believes in Me, though he were dead, yet shall he live again.*'[11] Articus, you never may understand all the 'Whys' about *Yahweh* or *Yeshua*. But ultimately, you must trust in *Yahweh's* declaration about Himself.

"Sir," asked Artie, "if I were to accept by faith what you and the others have told me about *Yeshua*, how will it affect my life? I've heard that Rome sometimes puts soldiers to death who have become his followers. Is that true?"

Responding, Cornelius said, "It has happened in some instances but not to those stationed as far from Rome as we are. However, Peter and others have warned me that believers should be prepared for some persecution because of our faith, which he said was 'sharing in the suffering of *Yeshua*.'"[12]

"What about other things in my life? On my way from Jerusalem I walked with two soldiers who thought I had gone 'soft' because I was interested in *Yeshua*." They suggested I would be too timid and afraid to fight for the Emperor like a true Roman soldier. Do you agree? Can one be a soldier and fight an enemy to the death and still be a follower of *Yeshua*?"

"Articus, from what I have learned about *Yeshua's* teachings, He taught that government is appointed by *Yahweh,* and that soldiers are His *'ministers of justice.'* One of our purposes is to keep law and order, and to punish those who do wrong.[13] From my understanding, that would include even to the point of death."

"What about my personal life? Would I have to give up wine and enjoying a good time with others at the local tavern? What if I were to marry a Jewess?"

"Articus, these are things you will have to decide for yourself. As I told you a while ago, *Yahweh* will '*...give you a new heart and put a new Spirit within you.'* *Yeshua* said that the *Spirit* would *'guide you into all truth.'*[14] If you listen closely to the *Spirit* He will '*...convict you of sin and make you aware of God's righteousness...*'[15] Over time you will find your heart leaning away from the things of this world and longing to learn more about *Yeshua*.[16, 17]

"In addition, I will encourage you to meet with a local group of believers who come to my home every first day of the week after work to learn more about *Yahweh* and *Yeshua*. These meetings are not mandatory but are simply times when we pray and worship together and have fellowship with one another. Several of *Yeshua's* apostles, including Peter, have written detailed letters about a believer's relationship with him, and copies have been made and circulated throughout the region.

I have a copy of a letter Peter wrote which we are studying right now. As time passes, you will find yourself making new friends with these believers, who include several other soldiers from this garrison, and even preferring their company over others.[18] Then one day you will discover that you have become a 'new man made in the image of *Yeshua.*'"[19]

"Sir, I have one more question."

"Yes, Articus, what is it?"

"What happens when we die?"

"*Yeshua* said that when His followers die, they '*do not come into judgment, but pass from death into life*.'[20] He also said there will come a day when He will come with all of angels and sit on His throne. All the nations will be gathered before Him, and He will separate them as a shepherd separates his sheep from the goats. To those who have rejected Him, He will say, '*Depart from Me, accursed ones, into the eternal fire which has been prepared for the devil and his angels.*' But to those who have received Him, He will say: '*Come, you who are blessed of My Father, inherit the kingdom prepared for you from the foundation of the world.*'"[21]

"What do I have to do to become a follower of *Yeshua*?"

"The process is not complicated Artie. First, each one who has chosen to be a follower must examine his life and be willing to admit he has done things in his life and thought things in his heart that are harmful to himself and his fellow man, and hurtful to our righteous *Yahweh*.[22] Then he must make a conscious decision to turn from doing those things and seek *Yahweh's* direction in his life. He or she does that by taking this very simple step: '*Confess with your mouth Yeshua as Lord and believe in your heart that Yahweh raised Him from the dead, and you will be saved.'* "²³

"It's as simple as that?" asked Artie.

"Yes, the difficult task comes later as the *Spirit* helps you understand what is pleasing to *Yahweh* and pulls you back from those things which your old friends do and may continue to encourage you to do. As the apostle Paul wrote in one of his letters, '*The natural man does not accept the things of the Spirit of Yahweh, for they are foolishness to him; and he cannot understand them, because they are spiritually appraised.*'²⁴ He also said '*each one has to work out his own salvation with fear and trembling.*' Your unbelieving friends may ridicule or harass you with their words or actions, and that can be hard to take. Eventually either they will try to understand your new life in *Yeshua*²⁵ and want to know more about Him, or simply pull away to spend time with fellows who agree with them. Through the process you may lose some old friends but gain many more new ones among men and women who love *Yahweh* and find joy in living according to His teachings and commands."

"If *Yahweh's Spirit* leads me to become a follower, do I have to be with you or another believer when I do?"

"No, Artie. In fact, I would encourage you to think clearly about what you heard from all the followers you've met and the conversation we have had this afternoon. Then, if you make that decision to follow *Yeshua*, just say a simple prayer to *Yahweh*, asking Him to forgive you of your sins and to send His *Spirit* to come into your heart and become your guide. You can do that anywhere and at any time. However, I have found that when men make that commitment their hearts burst inside them with a desire to share their joy with someone else. Also, they want to know what steps to take next as new believers. Artie, it will be up to you as to whom you tell and from whom you seek counsel. Just remember, it would be a great personal joy to me if I should be the one you choose." With that closing comment Cornelius prayed for Artie's decision, and the two men parted company.

Notes

1. Between 9:00 p.m. and midnight
2. About 4:00 p.m.
3. Ephesians 1:5
4. A military acronym which stands for Absent Without Official Leave.
5. Matthew 28:1-4
6. Mark 9:24
7. 1 Corinthians 14:33
8. Ezekiel 36:26-27
9. Hebrews 11:1, 3
10. Ephesians 1:5
11. John 14:6
12. 1 Peter 2:20–21
13. Romans 13:1–7
14. John 16:13
15. John 16:8
16. 1 John 2:15
17. Philippians 2
18. Romans 12:10
19. Colossians 3:10
20. John 5:24
21. Matthew 25:31–41
22. Romans 3:23
23. Romans 10:19
24. 1 Corinthians 2:14
25. Romans 6:4

CHAPTER

36

WHAT SHALL I DO WITH *YESHUA*?

"We see Him who was made for a little while lower than the angels, namely, Jesus, because of the suffering of death crowned with glory and honor, so that by the grace of God He might taste death for everyone."

Hebrews 2:9

Leaving the centurion's office, Artie headed toward a small grove he had marked out as his quiet place not long after being posted to Caesarea. It contained a comfortable bench near an artesian spring, a place where one could sit and hear nothing but the quietly bubbling water and songs of birds. Once again the distinctive song of a *Yellowhammer* caught his ear. He remembered that Cornelius said some thought the song sounded like "a little bit of bread and no cheese." But as he sounded those words in his mind while the bird sang, Artie began to think they sounded more like "be born again and follow Me." As that thought went round and round in his mind, he then thought he could hear *Yeshua* saying "Artie, follow Me."

Finally, bowing his head, Artie said this prayer:

"*Yahweh*, I know my life has been filled with shameful actions and pride in myself. I don't know everything I've done that You call sin, but I know there are many for which I would be ashamed if my centurion and others knew about them. My desire since I was young has only been to prove how strong and capable I am and to make a name for myself for Rome and the Emperor. But after being exposed to the knowledge and teachings of *Yeshua*, I now realize that is not enough. When my youth and vigor are spent, I want to look back over my life and see something achieved other than battles won and struggles lost. I want the peace and sense of composure in my life that I see in Thomas, Peter, my centurion, and Abigail. I know they will come only from receiving *Yeshua* as my Redeemer and Savior. I cannot begin my life all over again, but if You will have me, I want to be born again and start a new life living as Your bondservant. I pray You will send other followers into my life to teach me Your ways and show me how to live life under Your care and guidance. I am asking You to replace the questions I've had about why I was born and for what purpose with the knowledge that it is to serve You and my fellow man. I know that receiving *Yeshua* as my *Messiah*, being guided by your *Holy Spirit* and from fellowship with other followers I can become more of the man You have always wanted me to be. Now and forever more I commit my very life to you. I am not sure exactly how faith works, but I will begin each day praying to You and asking Your *Spirit* to guide me through the day ahead."

As Artie finished his prayer, it seemed as though the Yellowhammer's song became more and more persistent. Then he remembered that in his cloak was the small scroll Abigail had given him when they parted. She had said

Yahweh's Spirit would tell him when to read it, and he felt as though *Yahweh* was using the Yellowhammer to tell him the time was now! Untying the delicate blue bow she had fashioned to hold it fast, Artie read this note:

"Articus, if indeed the *Holy Spirit* has spoken to your heart and instructed you to read this small scroll, I pray the words you read will give greater clarity to your decision. Please know that my brother and uncle have given permission for you to return here to visit, and the three of us will joyfully welcome you into the family of *Yahweh*."

Overcome with joy at Abigail's note, Artie began to read the scroll…

"*Our Father, Who art in heaven, hallowed be Thy Name…*"[1]

THE END

Notes

1. Matthew 6:9–13, "The Lord's Prayer"